The Good Girl

Alyssa Corbet

Copyright © 2024 by Alyssa Corbet

All rights reserved.

No portion of this book may be reproduced in any form without written permission from the publisher or author, except as permitted by U.S. copyright law.

Contents

1. Chapter 1 — 1
2. Chapter 2 — 5
3. Chapter 3 — 8
4. Chapter 4 — 13
5. Chapter 5 — 16
6. Chpter 6 — 19
7. Chapter 7 — 22
8. Chapter 8 — 25
9. Chapter 9 — 29
10. Chapter 10 — 37
11. Chapter 11 — 46
12. Chapter 12 — 55
13. Chapter 13 — 65
14. Chapter 14 — 72
15. Chapter 15 — 79

16. Chapter 16 — 86
17. Chapter 17 — 91
18. Chapter 18 — 98
19. Chapter 19 — 106
20. Chapter 20 — 110
21. Chapter 21 — 115
22. Chapter 22 — 119
23. Chapter 23 — 126
24. Chapter 24 — 133
25. Chapter 25 — 140
26. Chapter 26 — 145
27. Chapter 27 — 150
28. Epilogue — 156

Chapter 1

Alisha's P.O.V

Beep

Beep

Beep

"Ugggghhhh" I groan. I turn off my stupid alarm clock and stare at it. 6 o'clock. School is in 3 hours. But I like to get there early so I can avoid "the populars". I get out of bed and head for the shower. I strip of my clothes and let the water consume me. I love showers! Oh I guess I should tell you about myself.

Well my name is Alisha Johnson. I'm 16 and 5 foot 1. Yes I know I'm short but I don't care. My dad is loving and so is my mom. However they can be a little rude, but they really don't care what I do as long as I'm safe. My brother, he is the best. He's a year older than me and honestly I can't ask for a better brother. He's protective over me but not over protective. Yes I'm a good girl and a nerd. I get really good grades. Never under an A-. Well other than gym in which I got a B+. I'm hoping to go to Harvard Medical University so I can leave this town. Oh right, I live in a little town in California. Don't get me wrong, I love it here, but I want to explore places! But I will always love the boiling heat and un sleep-able nights (can you hear the sarcasm?)!

I get out of the shower and put on some clothes. My first day of school outfit consist of a black dress that goes down just above my knees. It has a floral print with roses and its spaghetti strap. I slip on my black converse and I'm ready to go.

My hair and makeup is very natural. I curled my hair into loose waves that fall nicely against my back. My hair is long and brown. My eyes are hazel brown and my skin is pale but a little tanned. For eye shadow, I put in a light, shimmery, gold that blends in with my skin. Then I go ahead and do a winged liner. I put mascara on, and light red lipstick, and then I apply some lipgloss. I smile at myself in the mirror. I admit I'm not pretty, but I'm not ugly. Let's say I'm...decent; or acceptable. But I'm very insecure.

I sigh and rush downstairs. I make myself a Nutella and bread sandwhich and eat it peacefully. I look at the time and it's 7:30. I get my things and wake up Mike.

"Mike. Mike! Mikey! Hey Mickey Mouse wake up! Walt Disney is here to see you!" I say while giggling.

"Huh? Walt Disney? What? Ugh!" He groans.

"Mike seriously! It's 7:30 and I want to leave in 45 minutes!" I say while shaking him.

"Oh fine! Ugh I hate getting up!" He says and sits on my bed. I smile at him and we hug.

"Yeah I know big bro," I say into his chest. That's when I realize he was shirtless. But i didn't really care because I've seen him shirtless many times. He had a 6 pack because he worked out so much.

He walks to his bathroom while I run downstairs. I take this time to check my social media. You know Instagram, Twitter, Snapchat! Not many people followed me; but that was because I wasn't popular like Mike. I didn't mind it though. I liked being unnoticed, most of the time.

After I'm done checking social media, I look at the time, 8:10. He should be down in 5 minutes. I flip on the tv and watch the news, then my eyes fall on a picture. It was me, my former best friend and Mike. When we were little. Her name is Nina.

Before you go all sad, chill. She is still alive! It's just, after Rebecca Patterson talked to her, well they became best friends, and she left me. We still talk and all, but not like we used to in freshman year. I miss her though. We were best friends since we were 3 years old! The one good thing is that she doesn't bully me and she tries to tell Rebecca not to bully me too. Tries. She still does.

I snap out of my trans when Mike calls me. His dark brown hair is all messy but it suits him. He was wearing jeans, a striped shirt and converse. Mike is my ride. Don't get me wrong, I have a licence but I prefer not to drive. I only drive on certain occasions.

We get into the black Lamborghini and drive to school. Yes we are rich but we don't have a ginormous house with maids and butlers. Our house is normal size. My parents are saving the money for university.

We park in the parking lot and get out. Mike has football practice so we hug and say our farewells and head our separate ways. I go to the library and unlock it. I know what you're thinking, did you steal the keys? No. The librarian, who likes to be called by her first name Anna, by people she likes (me), gave me the spare keys cause I get here early. She knows I'm responsible and when things aren't always great, we talk. Yes she is old...maybe in her 60? But she is strong. She is like my grandmother.

I head inside and study. I don't have a test or anything I just study for future references. I check the time and it's 8:50. I sigh. School will start in 10 minutes. That's when Anna came in. We greet each other and she hands me some coffee. That how we work. I unlock the doors and she brings me coffee.

I say bye and head off to my first class, math. Don't get me wrong I love math but it's hard. I get in my seat at the back. Where I can't be seen. I look over my homework and that's when the teacher comes in.

"Hello Ms. Johnson," he says.

"Hello!" I smile and respond.

Then all the other students come in. Chattering and laughing. I sigh. I used to be like that. But it all changed after freshman year. I see Nina and Becca talking and giggling. She sees me and smiles. I give her a small smile and then look away. I admit I'm mad at her. Even though I said I wasn't. I really was. But she doesn't know that. If I tell her she will hate me. I'm fine being a nobody. I just have to survive this last year of school and I'm out!

The teacher starts talking about math. Reviewing and what not. I just put in my headphones and listen to music. He knows I understand everything and that I get bored, so he just gives me worksheets and once I'm done I listen to music. Everybody gets up and gathers there things, that my signal that the bell has rung for second period. History, here I come.

Chapter 2

Alisha's P.O.V

The bell rung and I was out of English. I walk towards my locker. Once I get there I see Josh Campbell making out with a girl just 10 lockers away from me. I shiver in disgust. He was the player of the school. He is basically a legend. Yes he is the same age as me but no we don't talk. He doesn't even notice me. Thank God! I wouldn't want to be one of his...victims? I don't know. I get my books out for my next class after lunch and slam my locker shut. In the corner of my eye I look at Josh. He pushed the girl away and walked off. I guess he was finished with her. Time for another.

He walks in my direction and I look down on the ground, not wanting to make eye contact. However, I can feel him looking at me. I suck in a breath and look to the side. I was right he looked at me for..3 seconds and smirked. God I hate him. I'm never gonna let him get to me. My first kiss was reserved for the right person.

I rush off to Starbucks across the street. I get a pumpkin spice latte and go back to school. I don't do cafeterias. Thats where everybody talks about gossip and what not and the populars would just target me. I sit in the hallway alone. I'm fine with it. Really. I like the quietness. Then suddenly, I hear clacking. Just my luck it's Becca and her minions. Nina was there, and when she saw me her eyes widened with worry. I knew what was coming but I most definitely did not expect this.

"Hey Ughlisha!" Rebecca says in a high pitched voice. Her minions laugh, except for Nina.

"Rebecca," I say in almost a whisper.

"So all alone again? Being all innocent? Yeah I think not! I saw what you did. You just couldn't keep your eyes to yourself and you looked at Josh! And then he looked at you! Stay away from him cause he's mine!" She yells.

"First of all, I never wanted him to, look at me. Second of all I don't care if he's yours! Third of all..." But I couldn't finish. Becca just pushed me against the lockers, hard. Then her minions grabbed me.

Their were 5 of them, including Nina. 4 of them grabbed each part of my body. My arms and legs. I tried running away but their nails dug into my skin making it bleed. I hold back a whimper and just think of happy things. I looks at Becca and she looked mad. She comes closer and slaps me across the face, real hard. Then she punches me in the face almost a dozen times and then in the stomach till I fall to the ground. She kicks me at least 5 times and walks away. But not before pushing me against the lockers, again. I feel the bruises on my arms, shoulders, legs...basically everywhere. I couldn't stand up. I was to weak.

I've dealt with her before but never once has she been abusive. She usually just verbally bullied me, never physical. I lay on the ground helpless. I didn't bother trying to call for help or getting up. It was useless. But the worst part is, Nina didn't even care! She watched me get tormented. And then walked off with her new bestie. Suddenly I hear laughing and talking from guys.

Shoot I gotta get out of here! I think to myself.

I tried getting up but I ended up hitting my head against a locker and falling. Now I felt light headed but I urged myself to stay awake.

Come on Alisha be strong! Yes you haven't been hurt this badly before, but you gotta stay strong! Don't cry just breath. I told myself.

But each and every inch of my body ached. The footsteps and laughter got closer. But I could barely hear it, even if they were close. I knew I was going to black out but I had to stay strong.

"No way! She may look pretty but she was a terrible kisser!" One guy said.

I recognized the voice barely. Shoot! It was Josh and his friends! They turned the corner while one if his friends says:

"You've done better! Remember that girl..." But he trailed of. I knew they saw me. I saw blurred faces.

No Alisha! Stay awake! STAY AWAKE! I kept telling myself.

"What's the matter bro?" I hear Josh.

"Look behind you," his friend said pointing at me.

All 5 of his friends turned around. Including Josh.

"Oh My God," Josh said and ran towards me.

My vision was getting blurry almost to the point where I couldn't see. There was blood everywhere. Probably from Rebecca's, perfectly manicured, minions.

"Luca go tell the nurse to keep a bunch of medical things ready or whatever!" Josh yelled at the boy named Luca. He ran. Josh picked me up bridal style, and kept on looking at me. And then....I blacked out.

Chapter 3

Alisha's P.O.V

"Come over here you stupid little girl!" Says an angry looking guy.

"Please don't hurt me!" The little girl cries.

"Give me what I want and maybe I will spare you!" The man calls.

"But I can't! She's gone! I don't know how!" The little girl screams and starts to cry.

"Well, I guess you're out of luck then aren't ya?" The man says with and evil grin and laugh.

The girl starts to cry and whimper because of what was happening. And that's when I realized that little girl...was me. It was a memory I thought I burnt. But it looks like I didn't. It's still in my head.

It was a long time ago when my uncle lived with us. He was drunk and abusive. My parents went away a lot and he was the only one they could find. He was sober around them, but the minute they left he drank. I was 5 at the time. And Mike was 6. He knew what he did and asked our parents if he could go to his friends place. They always said yes. Me? Well I was to young. Mike never thought our uncle would do such a thing, to me at least, but he did. He used to slap me, scratch me, beat me up. Once he even burned me!

One day my parents came home early from a trip and wanted to surprise us. When they entered the house, they saw him drunk and punching me while I cried. Mike was trying to get him off. They called the police and they took him to jail. Obviously, my parents were happy but they didn't move. They told me I was safe and I didn't have to worry. However, he said he would come back. But it's been 11 years, no sign of him! But that doesn't mean I wasn't still hurt.

I have trust issues and stuff and let me just say, it's bad. I'm also insecure and all that, but I get all my anger out in my own...special...way. Before you think something terrible no I don't cut myself or hurt myself in any way! Well that's semi true...

Beep

Beep

Beep

What? What's that noise? Why can't I get up? What's going on?

Idiot! You blacked out remember??

Oh right! I thought to myself.

Well....wake up!

Ok ok! I said to myself.

I wake up. My heart beating faster, and sweat was dripping from my head! Probably from my nightmare. I look around and realize I am in the hospital. There was a nurse their and she smiled.

"Glad to know you're awake," she says.

"Yeah...why am I here? How long have I been out? Where's my family?" I ask.

"Oh you were really hurt and I guess the shock got to you. You've only been out a few hours. Nothing serious. They called, saying they were on a flight to Asia. And that they will be back in 2 months. But your brother came," she said.

I nodded. Typical. Of course they go to Asia. But I knew they only said 2 months so I wouldn't get worried. They are really staying there for 6 months. I over heard them talking. I sigh and look back at the nurse.

"Thank you. When may I leave?" I ask.

"Whenever you're ready. I can call your boyfriend in if you'd like?" She says.

Wait...what? Boyfriend! I don't have a boyfriend!

"Um who?" I ask confused.

She looks at her paper.

"Josh Campbell?" she says.

Oh. My. God. Josh? As in bad boy Josh?

"Uh ok..." I trailed off and he entered.

"Hey Alisha..." he says.

"Um hi?" I say or more like asked.

"How are you?" he asks.

"Why are you here?" I ask confused.

"Um, the guys and I saw you on the floor. We rushed you to the nurse, she told us to take you here," he says.

I nod. The bad boys of the school...helped me?

"Um, we may be bad boys but we do have hearts," Josh says with a slight laugh.

Dang it! I thought out loud.

"I spoke to your brother. I told him I'd take you home," Josh says.

I nod again and get out of the bed. He leads me to his car, a red convertible. I get in and he drives in silence.

"Mind telling me what happened to you at school?" Josh says breaking the silence.

"Why do you care?" I say a little harsher than I intended.

"Why do you keep dodging my questions?" He asks. I sit there silently. He smirks and we keep driving.

"It was just Rebecca," I told him.

"Patterson?" Josh asks in shock. I nod.

"Holy Jesus! You must be pretty strong because the doctors said that you almost died!" He says. I gasp. Died?! Like she almost killed me?! Oh I was gonna get her.

You can't stupid! You know if you do you will let out your secret! I say to myself.

I sigh. Yeah I'm right. We stop at my house and I get out. I say a quick thank you and run to the door. I enter the house and I see Mike running up to me. He hugs me and I let out all small ouch.

"Sorry sis! What the hell happened to you?" He asks looking at me.

"Rebecca..." I say weakly. Mike's face turns from concern to anger in a flash.

"Oh I'm gonna give it to her!" He says while walking to the door.

I grab his arm and tell him no. It will just make things worse cause she will spread a rumour saying I was an attention seeker. Which I wasn't. He sighed and obeyed me. I tell him I was tired and was going to bed. He hugged me and I went to my room. I get into my comfy pyjamas and slip into my comfortable bed. I sigh and look at the ceiling.

"Hey sis, I wanted to tell you thanks, for being with me and helping me through it, you were always my best friend," I say to myself just before I fall into a deep slumber.

Chapter 4

Josh's P.O.V

I left her drive way. That little girl has some sass and not to mention an attitude problem. How was she suppose to be the good girl? But then again, she has never broken a rule, she has good grades, she has never gotten into a fight and all that stuff. Ok now I remember why she is the goodie goodie of the school. I pull up into my driveway and open the door hesitantly. I check the time. Oh no! 10:05! They will kill me.

I open the door waiting for what's going to to happen.

"Boy! You are 5 minutes late!" I hear my dad cry.

"I know I'm sorry it's just.." I couldn't finish because he slapped me. Really hard.

"I don't care about your stupid excuses! Carly! Down here now!" He hollers to my mother.

"Is he back?" My mother screams. I flinch when I see her with her curling iron. Oh no they are really mad!

"Guys it's 5 minutes!" I say to them.

My father pushes me against the wall and lifts up my shirt. Dang I'm gonna get it. My mother inches towards me but stops and grins at my dad. They kiss. Yuck! I took this time to run away but I guess they were expecting that. My dad yanks me back to the floor and my mom burns me with her iron. I don't scream. Even though I want to. If I scream they will just laugh and do it again. Once she takes her curling iron of me, they walk away. Leaving me there with bruises and a burn. I stand up and head for the shower.

Once I am done my shower, I go to my room and change. Guess I'm staying with Luca tonight. I call him.

"Sup Bro?" He says.

"I'm coming" I say.

"Not again! Ok I will leave the door open," he says then hangs up.

I sigh. He is supportive but this is getting outta hand! I jump out of my window and run to his house. I open the door and walk upstairs to his room.

"Hey I'm sorry. I know I can't come here all the time," I say.

"Yeah, I know you do. My mom is getting mad. She is telling me I can't have you over 24/7. Even the other guys are saying that!" Luca says.

I sigh. I knew this day would come. I wish it didn't come so soon. I go over to the guys places once something like this happens. I would go to my older brother Jacob's place but he lives in downtown. And I'm usually to lazy to take my motorbike there.

I get into my bed and go to sleep. But I can never fall asleep on these days. I sigh and go in Instagram. I search up Alisha Johnson and I can't find her... So I look on the school Instagram page. Everyone follows it just to keep up with updates and stuff. I go into followers and try to find her.

I go up and down and all of the buttons are green. Indicating I follow each and everyone of them. Well other than this one girl who've I've never seen. She probably doesn't go to our school but I request her anyway. She looks like Selena Gomez but it's not exactly her. Her name was Ally Rhonson. I request her. I don't really care if I don't know her, I just need more followers. Whatever. I guess Alisha doesn't have Instagram. I put my phone away and look at Luca. He was out like a light. I close my eyes and 30 minutes later I finally fall asleep.

A/N

Hi guys! I know short chapter! Sorry! I'm having writers block but more chapters are coming your way! Just be patient!

Stay tuned!

Keep reading!

And bye!

Chapter 5

Alisha's P.O.V

I woke up again. But this time at 6:15. Dang! I slept through my alarm clock! I rush to my bathroom not wanting to take a shower. So I just wash my face and put some deodorant and a little spritz of perfume. I go to my closet and take out some jeans, a white tank top, an oversized, but comfy sweater, that said NEW YORK, a scarf and some Uggs. Yes I went from girly to comfy in 24 hours deal with it.

I get my workout bag and put in a sports bra, some leggings and a hoodie. I go downstairs, get some toast and walk out the door. I go to my car, a small purple Mercedes. I never really rode it but I wanted to go some place today so I needed my own car. I get into the drivers seat and head of to school.

I get to school at 8:00. Great 1 hour of peace. I open the library and go into my corner. I study for a math test I'm going to have at first period. I hear Anna come in and I rush for my pumpkin spice latte. I really needed the caffeine after yesterday's incident.

"Hi honey! Are you okay? I heard what happens yesterday," Anna says.

"Yes I'm fine Anna. Don't worry!" I say rushing of to class.

I get inside and quickly review my notes one more time. Then everyone walks in. I sigh and close my book. I see Nina and Becca walk in. Nina glances at me and gives me a weak smile, I just look away. I can't deal with her. I look through the corner of my eye and I see in her eyes that she's hurt. Yeah! Well so am I!

The teacher gives us the test and I'm done in 30 minutes. I hand it in and listen to my music. I look around and almost everyone is done. They were all on their phones. I didn't realize I was singing softly to myself until one of my classmates nudges me.

"Yeah?" I say.

"You have a good voice," she says.

I blush and thank her, just then, the bell rings. I gather my stuff and head out the door. My classes role by quickly and once lunch roles around I get scared. This time I decided to stay at Starbucks. I sit at one of the tables and go on my laptop. I check my phone and see I have a request from...Josh???? Oh, thank goodness it was in my school account. I accept him and cary on with my business. 30 minutes later I head back to school and to Chemistry. Just then, I see Josh sitting right beside my normal seat. I sigh and head over there.

Poke

Ignore it

Poke

Don't let it bug you

Poke Poke Poke

Sorry brain you lose this time! Attitude do your thing!

"What the heck do you want?" I whisper yell at Josh.

"Just wanted to ask you what you got for number 4!" He says.

I roll my eyes and pay attention to my work. Bad boy has to figure it out for himself. The class ends and the rest of the day is free period and study hall. I go to both of them and since I didn't have any homework nor tests, I asked if I could go to Starbucks. The teacher said yes and I was of.

If you didn't catch on, I love Starbucks! It's basically my life. I get a vanilla bean hot chocolate and head back to school. I enter the class room and everyone stares. They have been doing that all day! I mean I hate attention and no one noticed me before! I guess it was the whole accident thing. I sigh and go to my seat and play my music. Finally the bell rings and I run to the bathroom to change. I put on my hoodie and my Puma sports bra, and run back to my car. I reverse out of the parking lot and head to the forest making sure no one followed me. I park at the mall and walk to the forest.

Once I get there, I take off my hoodie, tie it around my waist, put my hair in a ponytail and run to the warehouse. I enter and just as I suspect, all 15 people are there. Yeah if you didn't know this about me, I'm a fighter. You may be thinking, what? The good girl fights? Yeah I do! I guess I should fill you in since you are probably very confused. Well let's start from the beginning shall we?

Chpter 6

Alisha's P.O.V

Well it all started back with my abusive uncle, Bob. Well at the time, I had an older sister named Stacey. She was basically my best friend and I was hers. She was 6 years older than me, which meant she was 12, but it didn't matter to us. I looked up to her. I loved her. Well Stacey was very...mature for her age. And Bob loved women who were much younger and matured for their age. While he was drunk he would hit on my sister but each time she would pull away. Of course Bob didn't like that so one day he decided to threaten her with me. Basically he would beat me up until Stacey would finally become his slave. She only did that cause she cared for me.

Well one day, Bob was asleep on the couch. Stacey and I had finished doing all his work and I was super tired. She told me to go take a nap while she made cookies for me and her. I told her I didn't want to leave her alone with him but she assured me that she'd be fine, and that she loved me. She kissed the top of my head and gave me a weak smile. So I did. Once I was asleep, something happened. Bob woke up, and was very angry that Stacey didn't make cookies for him. He got so mad...he did something unforgettable. He pushed Stacey inside the oven, closed it and turned it up to the max. She screamed in pain and I woke up because of it. I ran downstairs screaming her name but she didn't reply. Bob came and started beating me up. I screamed for Stacey but she never came.

That was also the day my parents came to surprise us. Once the police came and all, they smelt the oven. They opened it and inside was my older sister dead. Her body was burnt and her eyes closed. I screamed and Mike comforted me. The funeral was 3 days later. I was a mess. I didn't want to eat or sleep. I just wanted to go to school and get my mind of it. But most of all, I wanted my sister back. Nina and my other best friend Ally were there to support me. They said they'd never leave me like Stacey did.

Life went on but I was still a mess. By the time I was 10, I was so mad and angry at myself cause if I didn't go take a stupid nap, my stupid uncle wouldn't have killed my loving sister. I was mad and so I ran. I loved to run, and I still do. I ran as far as I could go. I ended up in an alley. I was scared and I heard people. I started to cry and the people found me. I thought I was going to die. Turns out they were just kids. Their names are: Chris, Edward, Ray and Delilah also known as Danger. The boys were 2 years older than me but Danger was only one year older than me. They asked me what was wrong and I told them everything. They listened and once I was done they took me to this warehouse. Where only a few people knew about it. It was a place to let out your anger and fight. I loved it here.

They taught me everything I know. But I had to keep it a secret. I couldn't risk anybody finding out. Not even my best friends Nina and Ally; she moved to the next town over before freshman year. But she found out anyways cause she followed me. We still have connection but it's hard. Anyways, I'm one of the best fighters. I'm basically the queen of this place. We call it the Underworld. And down here, I'm Dynamite. I give people tips and tricks and no one tries to challenge me, you know except Chris, Edward, Ray and Danger. But I always end up winning.

I've never told anybody about this place. I kept everything about it a secret. I even kept Danger, Chris, Edward and Ray a secret. Even though we go to the same school, when we see each other we give a small smile but never give ourselves away or else we will attract to much attention. But I treated them like my brothers and sister. We called ourselves the Rippers.

So that's my story. And you may be wondering why I didn't fight back Becca, well if I did, questions would have been asked. So I couldn't. My life was basically here in the Underworld. Nobody cared if you were small or anything. It just mattered that you let your anger out.

Chapter 7

Alisha's P.O.V

I enter the warehouse and everybody cheers! I haven't been here in 1 week! The Rippers come racing towards me! Danger comes and hugs me a little to tight and my bruises and cuts start to sting.

"Ouch" I say.

"Oh right I'm sorry! I heard what happened! I wanted to give that little brat a piece of my mind but I sadly couldn't with these idiots holding me back!" She says pointing to the guys. I laugh and one by one they each hug me.

"Dy, you gotta be more careful! You're our little sister! And we can't exactl[y] protect you 24/7!" Chris says. He's the oldest and so he's the most pro[tec]tive. Mostly with me.

"Chris I'm fine! I'm here to punch the bags and let all my anger o[ut]

"You won't be fighting today right?" Ray asks.

I nod. No way am I fighting with all theses cuts and bruise[s]

"Good!" Edward says. Ray and Edward are twins, if yo[u]

I go to the punching bag and start to hit punch and kick it with all my might. Once I was done, I cooled of with some crunches, sit ups, push ups and squats. To tone my body. Once I was done, I go get a drink, Coke.

"So? What's the plan Dynamite?" Danger asks.

"Well D, I'm gonna go home, watch Scream Queens and then catch up on Pretty Little Liars," I say.

They nod and hug me good bye. I head out the door and go to the old train tracks. I go here to think. I was just staying here for a few minutes, to clear my mind.

When did life get so complicated? I thought to myself.

When Stacey died... My brain replied.

Yeah...we miss her don't we?

Yeah we do. No matter how hard we try, we won't get over her...but we gotta move on! You have to move on! My heart says.

I sigh. Fine I will try and move on. I get up and go to the mall where my car is parked. I made sure I zipped up my hoodie and let down my hair so I look like my usual self. Trust me, just because I'm a fighter, does not mean I'm not still a good girl, I still am.

I'm about to go into my car when I hear someone call my name. I whip my head around and get slightly whip lashed.

"Ouch," I mumble to myself. I look around and see Josh running after me. Shoot! I don't want him seeing me like this! I look like a freak.

"Hey! What are you doing here?" he asks.

"Um...just window shopping!" I say nervously.

"Oh ok, so um I know this is crazy but could you give me a ride home? Luca had to leave early and he left me here..." Josh said.

I nod my head and he gets into the passenger seat. I put my bag in the back and get into the driver's seat. Once we were on the road I asked him a question.

"So you and Luca were here why?"

"Um, well, I wanted to get a new guitar, and I didn't have my bike or my car so he was my ride. He got a call from his mom saying he had to come home and I forgot he was my ride and well here we are," he says.

I nod still keeping my eyes on the road. We pull up into his house. He quickly runs out of the car and says a quick thank you. I look at him confused but brush it off. I look at the time and its 9:59 pm. I sigh and get back on the road.

When I get home, its 10:05. 6 minutes, not bad. I run upstairs not bothering to say hi to Mike, he was probably at a party or something. I kick of my shoes, and jump into bed while taking my hoodie off. Who cares if I had a sports bra on? I don't! I close my eyes and fall asleep instantly.

Chapter 8

Josh's P.O.V

I enter the house just before it hits 10. Thank god! No beating up today! I felt bad for rushing off like that with Alisha but I had too.

I take my shoes off and see my parents asleep on the couch, drunk. I sigh and head to my room. I take my shirt off revealing my 8 pack. I smirk at myself in the mirror and head to bed.

Alisha's P.O.V

I wake up and its 6 o'clock. I get up take a shower and put on some leggings, a black tank top and a white cardigan. I slip on some black ankle boots and put my hair in a side braid.

I go downstairs, get some frosted flakes cereal and head out the door. I hop into my car and its...8:40? Awe man! I won't have any time to read! I head into school at 8:50. I walk to math class until someone grabs me and pulls me into the closet. It was...Nina?

"Nina? What are you doing?" I ask her.

"Lila..." but I cut her off.

"Uh, no. You lost the privilege to call me that after you left me," I say with a snarl.

"Ok whatever! Becca is after you! She said that she will grab you at lunch and will do worse than she did the last time! This is a warning don't be alone! I gotta go," she tells me and runs away.

The bell rings, and I rush to class. Thank god I got there on time! And what did Nina mean don't be alone? Doesn't she know I have no friends except for Ally?! Once all my classes were done, it was lunch. I flinched. I rush of to my locker and some one taps me on the shoulder. I flinch and gulp. This is the end for me. I turn around stiff and I see Becca and her minions there mad...Nina is at the back worried. I sigh, well I had a good 16 years right?

"Oh you will pay you beep," no need to hear that word.

She's about the punch me and I close my eyes. Suddenly someone lifts by my shouldersand puts me down. I hear a bang that sounds like someone hit a locker. I open my eyes to see...Jace? He's one of Josh's friends. And Becca is there holding her fist.

"Get the hell away from her Patterson! Or else you'll have me and the rest of the guys to deal with!" he snarls at her. She narrows her eyes at him, he does the same. She huff, flips her hair and struts of like she was on a cat walk...her minions follow her.

I stand there in shock...

"Uh, thanks?" I say more like a question.

"No problem, Josh overheard her plan and sent me to watch over you," he says while taking me to the cafeteria.

"Um, I'm fine going to Starbucks" I say softly.

"No can do little miss, Josh wants to make sure you're okay. Chill none of us will tease you or anything in anyway," Jace says like he read my thoughts. Man! I wanted Starbies!!

We enter the canteen and everyone stares. Shoot I hate attention! Ok I don't hate it. I actually like it, but not to much like this! Jace guides me to the popular table.

"Um you said nothing about me eating here! I'm fine! He saw me! Now I want my coffee!" I say while trying to escape. I guess Jace got fed up with me because he lifts me and swings me over his shoulders. More people stare. Dang!

He isn't as muscular as Josh but almost. I hit his shoulders and kick him too. Everyone stares. I roll my eyes and keep on hitting him.

"Let me go you moron! I'm a human not a puppet!" I say hitting him. He doesn't even flinch! Finally he sets me down and I'm in front of the populars. They stop talking and stare at me. I'm just as shocked as they are. They shrug and continue on like I wasn't even there. I snap out of my thoughts when someone starts to talk to me.

"I see you're alright, did that son of a beep..." I didn't here the last word. Instead I plugged my ears and said.

"La la la la la! I can't hear you! I will not let my head be filled with those stupid words!" I say. He looks at me and laughs. I roll my eyes at him and he stops.

"Ok, well did Patterson do anything to you?" Josh asks.

I shake my head no. He nods and tells me to sit down. I hesitate, and so he pulls me down. Josh talks with all his friends while me? I sit their awkwardly. I tried making a run for it but Jace caught me. When the bell rung, I got up and ran to chemistry...well speed walked to chemistry.

Once I get to my class, I move to the back, then Josh comes in, looks for a place to sit and the only place is beside me. Lucky me! Note the sarcasm. This is totally a cliché like all those other books. He moves into his seat and smiles at me. I give a slight smile and just look at the board. This is gonna be a long 60 minutes...

Chapter 9

Alisha's P.O.V

"When one chemical mixes with another chemical it will cause a chemical reaction!" My teacher says. I mentally tell her duh! I knew that when I was 7! Josh kept tapping my shoulder and poking me. I finally had enough of it and responded.

"Darn it Josh! What the hell do you want?" I scream whisper.

"Just wanted to ask you if we could hang out later?" he says.

"What? No!" I whisper.

He keeps poking me.

Ignore! Ignore! Ignore.

Poke

Poke

Poke

God dang it! Attitude your turn!

I snap my head to the left leaving me slightly whiplashed.

"Ouch..." I say softly.

"Hangout with me Alisha! Please! You owe me after I saved from that bi-uh Becca!" He says. I roll my eyes at him. Must he do this to me? The guilt card! The favour card! The owe card! I sigh.

"Will you stop annoying me if I agree?" I ask. He nods.

I sigh again and agree.

"Ok we will meet after school at my house," I say.

"After school? How about 3? I got a detention..." he says. I roll my eyes. Of course he did!

"Fine! 3!" I say and let my attention go back to the boring teacher. Every so often I would look at the corner of my eye and catch Josh staring at me.

What is he staring at?

You! Idiot! My heart says.

Well its not like we are dating! He doesn't even like me!

Yeah but you do! And you want him too! My heart says.

Shut up! My brain says.

No you do! My heart says.

No you do! My brain says.

Great now they are arguing about a stupid guy!

"Who's arguing about which stupid guy?" Josh ask me. I freeze with my eyes wide. Shoot! He heard! Curse my thinking out loud!!

"Oh no one!" I say and continue listening to the teacher. That was to close...

Once the bell rings, I get my things together and head out. Finally! School is done! I mean I love school and all but sometimes I just want it to be over. I guess you guys are probably saying "oh she just wants to hang out with Josh!" Well you're wrong! I'm not one of those clichés types of girls. Yes this is sort of a cliché after the whole, bad boy saves good girl thing, but I don't believe in clichés!

I start my car and blast the music. My boyfriend a.k.a Justin Bieber, okay maybe not my real boyfriend, What Do You Mean comes on! I am IN LOVE with this song.

"What do you mean?"

"Oh oh oh oh"

"Whe you nod your head yes, but you want to say no,"

"What do you mean?"

I sing along and go head home. Unfortunately there was traffic. Dang it! I hate traffic. When there's traffic in my area, it takes at least an hour to clear up. I sigh, guess I will be here for a while.

Finally after an hour, I get home. I had texted Mike in advance. He said its fine. He was sick today so that why I took my car. I pull up into the driveway and see a motorcycle...

What is that?

It's a motorcycle you idiot! My conscious tells me.

Yeah I know! I mean who's is that?

Well go inside and find out!

I roll my eyes at myself and slightly giggle at the thought of me rolling my eyes at nobody. I get inside still smiling at myself and I see Mike and....Josh? Sitting on the couch screaming at the tv. I clear my throat and they both jump up. Talk about awkward! I laugh and look at the tv...basketball. Of course, sports! I sigh and look at the time 3:05.

"Why are you late princess?" Josh asks. Princess? Really? Is he seriously doing the whole cliché nickname thing? Well if he calls me it, I must act the part because I'm a drama queen anyways!

"A princess is never late! Her subjects are simply early!" I say. They both look at me and laugh.

"So we are your subjects?" Mike asks with a grin. I simply nod and head upstairs.

"Um where are you going?" Josh asks.

"Um...going upstairs to change and go on my run..." I say confused.

"Um forget that you had plans with a certain handsome man?" Josh says. I took this opportunity to tease him.

"Um, Justin Bieber isn't here..." I say with a smirk. Josh gives me the don't-get-smart-with-me face. I laugh and go upstairs. Minutes later I'm downstairs in a pink sports bra, some shorts and my hair is in a slick back high ponytail. I have some abs, you can see them but They aren't really visible like Mike's. But I mean, at least I got them! I get my IPhone 6s and put in my headphones. I'm pretty sure Josh left...but I was dead wrong. I turn around and see Josh looking at me with his jaw open. He was checking me out!

"Close your mouth, you don't want flies getting in there do we?" I say patting his cheek and walking of with a grin.

"Wait you were serious when you said you were going out for a run?" Josh asks surprised. I nod and head out the door. Suddenly, Josh runs up beside without a shirt on. Leaving him in his shorts. I stare at his 8 pack....damn!

"Quit staring! It's creepy!" Josh says with a smirk I roll my eyes. Him and his cockiness! We run for a good 20 minutes. My music goes to the song Wildest Dreams by Taylor Swift.

"Say you'll remember me! Standing in a nice dress staring at the sunset babe!"

"Red lips and rosy cheeks! Say you'll see me again even if it's just in your..."

"Wildest Dreams!"

I sang my little heart out. We stop at a nearby bench to catch our breath. Josh taps me and says

"You have a good voice princess"

I blush. "Thanks but no I don't. My parents are ashamed that I can't sing, they say I'm worse than a dying seal..." I say shyly. Why did I just say that? Oh my god I swear I'm losing it! I mean it's true but I didn't need to say that!

Ok so maybe when I said my parents are loving...I was lying? Yeah I know. I'm bad! They actually used to be really mean to me. Never in a physical way...only once. Anyways they would put me down and what not and they wouldn't even care if I got hurt or something! Only Mike was there for me. That's why they usually went on business trips and all. It all started after Stacey died. I guess they blamed me...and I sort of do too. But no way was I going to tell Josh that!

"Hey! No way are you bad! You have a voice the sound of an angel! Your parents are dead wrong!" he says. I blush again. Why does he have to say sweet things like that to me?

He heads of to the Porta potty and I look around. No one was watching. I played a random song and danced. I love to dance. I've been practicing and taking a few lessons at school. It's one of my favourite ways to release stress! You know...after fighting. I kick my leg up, do some pirouettes, some jumps and all sorts of stuff. When the song ends I turn around to see Josh clapping. Aw man he saw me....AGAIN! I blush like a tomato.

"So...you're a dancer and a singer?" he asks.

"Me? No way!" I say. "I'm terrible."

Josh shakes his head.

"Please! Don't lie to me!" he says.

I shake my head and drop the subject. I start to run. Josh comes up beside me. He stops and I look at him with a questioning look.

"You, me, race to that big oak tree over there," he says pointing to the oak tree. Oh I love races! I'm pretty fast for my height and I've only been jogging. However, I think Josh thinks he can beat me. He'll just have to wait and see me sprint! Not run, sprint! I nod my head.

"Ok 1, 2, 3 go!" he screams.

I jog while he runs, soon I see him getting tired and I take this to my advantage. I sprint as hard as I possibly can and pass him in seconds. 30 seconds later I'm at the tree panting. Wow talk about a workout! Finally, after a few minutes, Josh makes his way to the tree. I smirk.

"What took you so long Bad Boy?" I ask giggling.

"For a short stack like you, you're pretty fast!" he says while panting. I grin.

"Why thank you!" I say bowing down. We both laugh. Suddenly I here the ice cream truck!

"ICE CREAM!" I shrieked. I run over jumping up and down like a child. But then I stop. Dang I have no money!!!! I frown and walk back to Josh.

"Wow, you really like ice cream," I nod. He looks at me questioningly.

"Um, so where is it?" he asks.

"Broke as f" is all I say. He laughs, takes my hand and drags me to the truck again.

"Don't torture me! Please!" is all I say. He chuckles.

"Princess, I'm getting ice cream for you," he says.

My eyes lite up like fireworks and I start jumping up and down. He asks what I want.

"Um....can I get a chocolate sundae?" I ask. The ice cream man nods...

"Oh what I ain't done. A sundae with chocolate sauce, hot fudge sauce, caramel sauce, chocolate chunks, chocolate sprinkles, chocolate chips, m&ms, and a bright red cherry on top," I say matter-of-factly. They both look at me stunned.

"Wow. The only thing you forgot is sprinkles!" Josh says.

"Oh that's what I was missing! And since I'm adding stuff, add whatver chocolate you have in there too!" I say.

The ice cream man shakes his head and makes my ice cream. I catch Josh staring at me with wide eyes and a shocked face.

"May I help you?" I ask.

"What? Oh no. Its just for a small, tiny and fit person like you...you sure eat a lot," he says.

I laugh. "Well I love ice cream! And chocolate. As you can see. But I run, exercise daily and fi-uh fire a lot of energy!" I say. Dang that was to close! I almost let out my secret!

"Yeah, I see," Josh says. The ice cream man gives me my ice cream and Josh pays. 6:79$. Oops!

Chapter 10

Alisha's P.O.V

We head back to my house and it was getting dark. 9:30 to be exact. When I finished my ice cream we went to the park and Josh pushed me on the swing. It was so much fun. Then we went out for dinner and...here we are! We were upfront of my house, and I had my sweater on. Josh smiles at me, I smile back.

"Well today was fun! But I gotta go, I hope we can do this another day!" he says. I knew it was a lie though. His buddies were probably busy and that's why he came today. But I went with it.

"Yeah! Totally! Well....bye!" I say. He walks to his motorcycle and starts the engine. He rides off and I enter the house extremely tired. Mike's car was gone so he was at a party. Probably staying the night. I sigh and go to bed.

I wake up to the sound of my alarm and groan. Another day of school. Thank god it was Friday! I get out of bed and pick out my outfit. A blue dress that goes down to my knees. Its patterned on the top and plain blue at the bottom. I paired it with a brown belt. (Picture above).

I put on my ankle boots, and walk to the bathroom. I brush my teeth, curl my hair, do a little bit of makeup and head downstairs.

Mike was up, thank god! Guess he didn't stay the night.

"Hey sis! You ready?" he asks. I look at my phone. 8:20. I nod. He drives to school and we head our separate ways. I decided to go to Starbucks and order a pumpkin spice latte. My usual. I sip my coffee and walk back to school. Suddenly someone hands are on my waist. I turn around and see Josh???????

"Uh hi?" I say more of a question.

"Hey Princess!" he says. I roll my eyes. Princess....that's what my parents used to call me.

"So...what are you doing here?" I ask. We were in front of Starbucks.

"I saw you sipping your coffee and decided to come up to you," he says. I nod.

"Ok well nice seeing you...bye!" I say turning around. He laughs and grabs my wrist.

"Come on Alisha! We can be friends!" Josh says. I flinch at the word. Friends. No I can't! No way am I trusting anybody.

"Us? Friends? Josh this is reality! You're the bad boy, I'm the good girl. We don't mix. You're popular I'm a loner! No one cares about me and that's how it has always been! Its sweet that you want to be friends but lets get real here. Who wants to be friends with me? I gotta go. See you around," I say and walk away. I know I know cliché right? Well to bad! The cliché thing stops here. I won't see him anymore and that's that.

I enter school and head to my first class. Hopefully lunch roles be fast!

Ding ding ding!

Yes lunch! Starbucks here I come! I run outside and head for Starbucks. When I enter, I see my order already waiting for me! I smile at the worker lady and pay her. They know me so well! Suddenly I see Josh and his friends walk in. Of course! I sigh and sit at a booth hoping they wouldn't see me. Nope they did.

Luca walks over to me and smirks.

"Hey Princess!" he says. Great all of them are calling me that now!

"Hello Luca," I simply say and sip my hot chocolate. He sits in front of me and calls all 4 guys over. Yay me! Note the sarcasm. There was Josh, Luca, Dylan, Chad and Jace. Josh and Dylan sit beside me, while Jace and Chad sit beside Luca.

"Oh look at the time! Gotta head back to school!" I say trying to make a run for it. I manage to get out of the booth but my waist is pulled back by Josh.

"Princess, we have 30 minutes left. Chill," he says. I sigh. Suddenly I realize I'm on his lap! Dang it! Cliché moment! I blush and luckily no one notices it.

I sip my last sip of my hot chocolate and hear my name.

"Alisha! Your chocolate donut and milk shake are ready!" the lady says.

I squeal and head for the counter. I throw away my cup and get my things. I go back to the booth eating my donut and sipping my milk shake. The guys look at me.

"Damn man! When you said she loves chocolate you weren't kidding!" Jace says. I practically choke! He talked about me to his friends? I blush.

"Yeah he did," Chad says with a smirk. Dang did I say that out loud?

"Um yeah you did," Dylan says. I blush even more. Curse my thinking out loud moments! The guys laugh and I roll my eyes. I finish my donut and head out the door hoping to get away from them.

"You son of a beep," I hear Rebecca say. Oh no! I turn around to see her very mad!

"You are trying to die right? Well its working cause I'm gonna kill you for hanging out with my boyfriend!" she screams in my face. Oh shoot I'm dead! That's not a metaphor!!!

She raises her fist but it doesn't make contact with me. I open my eyes to see Luca holding her back while Josh is in front of me with his arms out so she can't get to me. Jace, Chad and Dylan are holding her henchmen back.

"Let me say one thing to you Rebecca. Listen to me well and listen to me good. You mean nothing to me! You are not my girlfriend and I'm not your boyfriend. I can date whoever I want and its my life! So don't mess with Alisha because I swear I will kill you and all your minions if you do anything to her! Got it? Get it?" he says. She gulps and nods.

"Good. Glad we had this little chat!" Josh says. Luca lets go of her and the rest lets go of Rebecca's minions.

"Thank you," I say once they face me.

"No problem. We should probably get back to school. Study hall starts in 5," Josh says with a shrug. And we walk off.

School was finally done and I went home to change and go to the Underworld. I get into ny car and ride off. When I get into the warehouse I see the Rippers looking at me with sorry eyes. I walk over to them with a confused face.

"You guys okay?" I ask while ordering a coke. They shake their heads no. I look at them confused.

"Alisha we have some...good and bad news," Chris says. I nod.

"Ok well, us 4 have photography class together and we went into a competition earlier in the summer. We didn't think we would win but we did," Danger says. I smile with joy!

"Wow that's great!" I say congratulating them.

"Yeah but our prize is going abroad to study," Ray says. My smile slowly falls. Abroad?

"And we will be studying in...Paris!" Edward says. I gasp. Paris? Like Paris, France? Oh my god!

"Wow! That's...great! I'm happy for you guys," I manage to say holding back a sob. No I will not cry. I haven't in 6 years I'm not starting now.

"Dy, you don't have to say that. We know you're upset," Edward says. I nod.

"Guys this is an awesome opportunity! I will not let you guys miss it just because of me! We have technology for a reason! We can text, call, skype! And I can come to visit! I have family in Paris! I've never been there but I've met them! Please if you don't go I will be so upset!" I say.

"Really Lila?" Ray says. Yes they call me Lila. I nod. They hug me while Danger cried. I hugged her and calmed her down.

"So...when are you leaving?" I ask.

"3 days," they say together. I nod.

"Is this the last time I'll see you guys?" I ask sadly.

"Well for 2 years yeah. We will be packing our stuff so we wont be at school," Chris says. I nod and sigh.

"Okay! Well I guess this is a...see you later then!" I say with a small smile. They smile back a we get a group hug in and take a bunch of pictures and selfies. Yes we follow each other on social media. It was 10:30 and I had to get home. Wow, I won't be seeing my best friends for...2 years! Then I remembered something!

"Oh guys! I have a surprise for you! I kept on forgetting to give it to you guys!" I say. I pulled out 5 bracelets from my pocket. I give them to each of them and then one for myself. They all say The Rippers.

"They are friendship bracelets. I got them a few weeks ago but forgot to give them to you," I say with a small giggle. They laugh and hug me.

"Thanks Dy! We love them!" Danger says as she hugs me. Ok now I really have to get going.

I hug each of them individually.

First was Danger.

"Bye D. Love ya." I say.

"Love you too Dy. Whenever you need me, call okay? I will come back for you. We all will." she says. I nod.

I hug the boys. Edward, Ray then Chris. Edward kisses my cheek. Ray kisses my nose and Chris kisses my forehead.

"See you later little sis," Ray says.

"Stay safe! We love you!" Edward says.

THE GOOD GIRL

"If you ever need anything call okay? We are here for you. You're our little sister. If you're in trouble we will be there. We will come back for you in less than a heart beat!" Chris says. I nod.

"Yeah I know. Take care of D for me. She can be a handful." I say.

"Hey! I'll be fine! But Alisha try and let someone in. They can fix you. Stop shutting people out okay? Try!" Danger says. I sigh and nod.

"I will try! Bye sis and big bros! I love you and I will miss you!" I say with a little sadness. We do a group hug together for the last time. Then I head out. I look back, smile and raise my hand with my bracelet. They do the same. We all say Rippers! And then I leave. I'm gonna miss them so much. I hope they will too. That's when I realize, the 4 people who said they wouldn't leave me...are leaving. I sigh and walk to my car. I park the car, get inside the house and walk into my room. I fall on the bed and read a book on Wattpad.

Josh's P.O.V

Damn! Its 10:10! I'm screwed! I walk inside and suddenly I'm greeted with a punch to the jaw. It hurt like hell! Then I was slapped into the face. I was punched 10 times in the stomach and 20 times on each side. My mom got a boiling pot of water and poured it on my stomach I stayed strong and didn't scream. When thet were done, they laughed and headed straight for the door, to a club.

It took me at least 15 minutes to get to my room because my body ached. I got all my clothes together and went downstairs and out the door. I couldn't go to the guys place because they said their parents were getting suspicious. I had one place in mind...hoping they would let me stay.

Alisha's P.O.V

I was reading my book when I heard a tap at the window. I thought it was the tree but I guess I was wrong.

"Princess open up please!" I hear Josh's voice, but in pain. I go to my window seat and open my window to see a really badly beaten up Josh with a duffel bag. I gasp. I let him in and set him on the bed. I got the first aid kit and ran to his side.

"This will ache like hell but bare with me. After this terrible beat up and the drive and the climb here, you can possibly die. So do not argue with me!" I said in a stern voice. He was about to say something but I cut him off.

"No! Don't talk! It will waste to much energy. Just focus on breathing," I say. He groans and sticks to my instructions.

I clean his wounds with rubbing alcohol which he groans too. I get ice, cold water and put it on his burns. How the hell did he get these bruises?! I won't bug him about it, its his life. He will tell me when he's ready. And it would be too cliché...

After 45 minutes of him suffering, I was done.

"Ok I'm done. I see you have a duffel bag, want me to bring you to Luca's place?" I ask.

"No need princess. I'm exactly where I wanted to be," he says. I look at him with a confused face. Wait...he didn't just come here for a ride? Or for assistance? He actually came here for the night?

"I know what you're thing. Yes I would appreciate it if I could stay here for a few nights..." he says.

"Um...ok? Do you want to call home?" I ask.

"No! Don't!" he exclaims. I jump back at his reaction. What happened?

"Uh ok. I don't mean to be noisy and if you don't want to tell me don't worry about it...but what happened?" I ask then suddenly regretting it! Cliché much? What happened to the don't say anything plan?

"You know what sorry that was personal you don't need to answer. You will have the bed I will take the floor um...yeah I will let you change," I say quickly. Thank god I was in my pajamas. A white crop top that says 'Sweet Dreams' and some pink short shorts. But not to short...

"Alisha! Its ok...I will tell you," Josh says. I shake my head.

"Josh! I don't want you to feel pressured into telling me. That's your life, its ok," I say with a smile. He smiles back.

"I want too," he says. I sigh and sit on the bed in front of him.

"Okay, I'm listening," I say.

Chapter 11

Josh's P.O.V

"Okay...here I go. It all started when I was 3. I have an older brother name Jacob who is 3 years older than me, so he's 20. Anyways, at the time we had parents. But they did drugs. They knew what they were doing but they couldn't stop. So they put us up for adoption so they could go to Rehab. I was confused but Jacob, he was pretty mature for his age, so he knew what was going on. Well we were sent to this family, the one I'm living with now, and at first they were great! Until I hit 13 and Jacob was 16. They started harassing us and being abusive. It wasn't that bad because Jacob always told them off for us. Then he graduated and left for College. Luckily he's in downtown. Well they started abusing me even more and that was when I was 16. So last year. At first it wasn't that bad, just a few bruises. But today...today was bad. I have never been 10 minutes late and well you see what happened. But before I would always go to the guys place but their parents got suspicious so now I'm here. And I'm grateful you're letting me stay," I said. Alisha stayed quiet the whole time. She smiles when I'm done.

"I'm sorry you've had a rough past. I hope you work through it. And you're welcomed here anytime," she says.

Wow. I never knew a person could be so nice!

Alisha's P.O.V

Wow, his life was almost like mine! I sigh and get up.

"Well its uh getting late, we better get to bed," he nods. I was a about to walk to the door but Josh grabbed my hand.

"Where are you going?" he ask.

"Um...I'm getting some pillows and blankets for my bed..." I say. He shakes his head.

"Um no. Your bed is already ready," Josh says pointing at the bed.

"Yeah that's where you're sleeping," I say.

"And you!" he says. I look at him confused and then my eyes went wide.

"Oh no Mr. Bad Boy! We are not doing--" but he cut me off.

"Chill Princess! We are just sleeping side by side together!" he says. I sigh, no point in arguing. I get in beside Josh and snuggle with my teddy bear.

"Um don't you want to take of your makeup?" Josh asks.

"Um its all off," I say. He looks at my face.

"Holly shi-sheez, your face is flawless!" he says. I giggle.

"Thanks!" I say. And then I fall into a load of darkness...

You think you're so innocent? Well you're not! You are big, at and ugly! I can't believe I was stupid enough to call you my friend. No my best friend! I just needed a girl best friend but now I don't. So you can run along Loser! I don't need you anymore!

"Stacey? STACEY?"

"She isn't here sweety! She's probably dead by now! Your turn!"

"You're stupid, ugly, crazy and we are ashamed to call you our daughter!"

I jolt up gasping for air. I'm sweating all over! My head throbbed and I felt a few tears come down. I wipe them away and silently scolding me for almost letting all the tears out. Josh wakes up to see me breathing heavily and I look like a mess. I sobbed.

"Hey? What's wrong?" he says stroking my hair.

Open up to him! Do what Danger told you! My heart tells me me. I sigh.

"Its time I open up to you. At this point you're the close's thing to a friend as I have..." I say.

"Hey! You don't have to tell me anything! Not if you aren't ready" he says softly. I shake my head.

"No I'm ready right now," I say. He nods and I tell him about Stacey and the night when I was 10.

"My parents got mad at me for the littlest things. So one day I forgot to call them that I'd be staying at Nina's house. Yes Nina Robinson. Anyways, when I came home they abused me and burnt me along my arm. That's why they go out a lot, so they can stay away from me. I guess thy blamed me for Stacey's death. And to be honest so do I. I ran away and 4 kids found me...Chris, Ray, Edward and Delilah. They helped me through it and we treated each other like brothers and sisters. Of course I am the youngest but I'm pretty tough," I say.

"Yeah I know them! They won that competition..." Josh says.I nod.

"So that's my story, you would think after 12 years I would have gotten used to the nightmares...but nope!" I say.

"First of all, you aren't ugly, you are beautiful. Second of all, I'm sorry for your lost, but I know for a fact Stacey wouldn't want you blaming yourself for her death! And can I ask you a question?" he says. I nod.

"Well after that nightmare, why didn't you cry? I mean that was pretty brutal if you ask me!" he says. I sigh and tell him.

"After that night when I was abused, I cried and cried and cried. It looked like I was a weakling! So I stopped crying. I pulled myself together and promised myself I wouldn't cry. I haven't for 6 years! And I'm not planning to anytime soon," I sigh. He nods.

"Well I just wanted to tell you that I'm your friend and so are the guys. You can talk to us about anything except for...personal things....if you know what I'm getting at," he says with a smirk. I giggle and nod. But I knew he was lying. He was saying theses thing to make me feel better...

"Thanks... But I'm telling you right now, I have EMENSE trust issues and I'm insecure. So don't take it personally if I'm sort of...distant," I say. He chuckles.

"Don't worry princess," is all he says. I smile. I look at the clock, 5 am...Well I'm suppose to wake up in an hour anyways so I decided not to go back to bed. I go take an extra long shower. I come out and Josh is asleep. I go to my closet and pick out my outfit, tights, a pink crop top and a hoodie. I go back into the bath room and change. When I get out I see Josh frowning.

"Damn it! I wanted to see you change!" he grunts. I roll my eyes. Perv much! He chuckles and gets out of bed. I didn't realize he was only in his boxers. I turn my head, not wanting to stare...

"Oh come on princess! You know you can't resist me!" he says walking towards me. I shake my head and blush.

"Princess?" he asks.

"Prince?" I respond. Yes I know cliché. He chuckles.

"Prince?" he says back. I nod.

"Well, we should go and get some breakfast," he says. I nod.

"Ok I will cook!" I say. He shakes his head no.

"Actually I am making the food," he says. I look at him confused.

"No you are the guest...so I make the food!" I say. He shakes his head no again.

"Exactly I'm the guest that busted through your window asking if I can stay here because of my problems! So the least I can do is make breakfast for you!" he says. I look at him with a really-I'm-trusting-your-cooking face.

"I make some pretty delicious pancakes!" He says. I giggle. For some reason he can always make me laugh when I'm down. I sigh and nod my head. He grins, picks me up and spins me around. I laugh. We go downstairs and enter the kitchen. He starts the pancakes while I get the juice.

"So, whats the plan?" Josh asks.

"Um...school? You go with your friends and I go to the library..." I say. He laughs.

"Oh I'm not going to school. I'm ditching with the guys," he says.

"Um ok...well I better get going because I'm gonna walk then," I say. He looks at me confused.

"Oh I would take my car but its out of gas," I say.

"Uh I will drive you on my motorcycle," he says. I shrug.

"K I will meet you down here in an hour, after I eat," I say. It was 6:30 and I munched on my pancakes.

"Wait? You're not scared?" he asks. I shook my head no.

"Wow, you're not like the other girls. All the girls I've been with were always scared to ride my bike," he says. I laugh.

"Not this girl! I'm not afraid. See you at 8!" I say then running upstairs.

It was 7 o'clock. I go upstairs and change into jeans, a crop top and my black heels. I straighten my hair, and let it fall loose. Then I put on my makeup. Some concealer, a wing eye liner, mascara, red lips and eye shadow. It was 7:45 when I was done. I sigh and get my things together. I get downstairs and what for Josh. At 7:59 I call Josh.

"Campbell! Hurry up!" I yell.

"Chill Princess! I'm coming!" he yells back.

He comes down wearing jeans, a white shirt, and converse. He looks at me with his mouth open. I look down at myself.

"Oh god! Do I look bad? Dang I knew I shouldn't have worn this top!" I say frustrated.

"Oh no! Alisha you look...stunning," he says. I blush. God why? He's a player! I can't get close to him. Yeah I opened up to him but only because Danger told me too.

"Uh thanks. Can we go now?" I ask. He nods. We head out the door and we get onto the bike and ride to school. The wind rushes through my hair. Its so freeing! We stop and I was sort of sad because I liked the feeling.

"Here we are Princess," I get of the bike and go inside the school. I look back to see Josh staring at me. I sigh go inside and head into Math class. I look through my notes and wait for the day to be over! And then I realize one tragic thing....I forgot my Starbucks!

Ding

Ding

Ding

Yay! Home time! No! Walking time! I sigh. Maybe I shouldn't have took up Josh's offer. And sigh and walk out the school doors. Just then I hear someone call my name.

"Alisha!" I hear a voice. I turn around and see....Ally?

"Ally???" I scream. We run to each other and hug. I haven't seen her in 6 months!

"Oh my god! Al? What? Why? How?" I ask.

"I'm have a holiday and decided to visit my hometown!" she says. Just then somebody calls Ally's name. We both turn around and see Nina.

"Ally? Oh my god! I've missed you!" she says. Ally smiles. She knows what Nina did to me and now she doesn't really consider her as a friend.

"Uh yeah hey Nina. Its um...nice to see you," she says. "I guess," she mumbles under her breath. I but my lower lip to stop from laughing.

"Look guys! I know I'm a bit of a bad person for leaving you guys but you can't blame me!" she says. We look at each other and sigh. The only reason she left me was because she wants to become famous. So when Rebecca offered her a place in the popular group, she took it in an instant. Thats one step closer to becoming a celebrity right?

"Yeah ok whatver Nina," Ally says. She grabs my hand and walks me to her car. In the distance we hear Nina yell.

"We were best friends! You can't change that!"

We roll our eyes. We get into Ally's car and drive to my house. We enter the house and see Mike sitting on the couch watching Football. Sports again...

"Hey Alisha. And....ALLY?" He says. He jumps up and brings her into a big bear hug. She laughs and hugs back.

"Hey how have you been?" Ally asks.

"I'm good. You?" she responds.

"I'm great! Just came to visit my two favorite people!" she says. We laugh and head upstairs into my room.

"So how have you been girl?" she asks.

"Well, nothing new. Just the bad boy, Josh, has started talking to me," I say and she gasps!

"Wow!" she says. I roll my eyes.

"Any news on...Zack?" Ally asks.

"Nope nothing since sophomore year! That's how I like it!" I say. She nods.

"The Rippers?" she says.

"They all moved to Paris to study abroad. They will he back in 2 years though..." I say.

"Alisha I know you are hurt and I'm here for you," Ally says.

"Yeah ok. Lets just forget it okay?" I ask. She sighs and nods. We talk and laugh for hours. Until she has to leave. I sigh. We won't see each other for another 6 months. But we talk on the phone.

"Bye Alisha, love ya!" she says and hugs me. I hug her back.

"Bye Al. Love ya too," I say.

She heads out the door and gets into the car. She waves at me and drives off. I sigh and head upstairs where I see Josh on my widow seat. It was 8 o'clock.

"Hey," I say sitting on my bed

"Hey princess," he says. I grab my guitar and play a few songs.

"You play?" he asks. I nod.

"Same," he says. I look up and smile. I look at the time and see its 11 o'clock. I sigh and put my guitar away.

"I'm gonna go to bed. Will you be coming home everyday at 8?" I ask while getting into bed. He nods.

"Ok well good night. Are you going to bed?" I ask. He nods and climbs in beside me. I fall asleep in an instance.

Chapter 12

Alisha's P.O.V

I wake up at 6 on my own. No alarm today! My body is just naturally used to waking up at this time. I try getting up but something was keeping me down. I look down and see a muscular arm wrapped around my waist.

"Josh?" I say. He shifts around but doesn't let go.

"Josh?" I say again. He mutters something that I didn't catch but still holds onto my waist.

"Josh! Let go! I need to take a shower!" I say trying to take his hands off, but he only holds on tighter. I sigh.

"Come on Princess! You smell fine! 30 minutes more, please?" he says in a hot, and husky morning voice. Wait did I really just think that?

"Ok fine," I say giving up and trying to go back to sleep, but I can't. That's just me. When I wake up I can't go back to sleep.

"I can't get to sleep either, wanna play 20 questions?" Josh says. I swear that boy can read my mind. I nod and turn around so I'm facing him.

"Ladies first!" he says. 20 questions? Me going first? All cliché! I think of a question and decide to go with the one everybody chooses first.

"Favourite colour?" I ask with a smile. He laughs and responds.

"Blue, you?"

"Pink," I say. He chuckles.

"Favourite singer?" he asks.

"Justin Bieber, no brainer!" I say with pride. I don't care what he has done! Whatever he has done made him the person he is today.

"Wow. So you're a Belieber?" he asks. I nod.

"Why haven't you called the cops on your....adoptive parents," I ask. He shrugs.

"If I do, I will have to move in with my brother. I will be to much work for him and I will have to move schools. I will live with it for another year. I'm turning 17 in February so I will be fine," I nod.

"Well you can stay here till you turn 18 if you want. I mean, you can go back home but whenever you need a place to stay, you're always welcomed here," I say. Even though I think that he is only pretending to be my friend, I will be his real friend. And friends help each other out...even if one of them is just pretending.

"Thanks Princess," he says and smiles. I smile back.

"Your welcome Prince," I say. He laughs.

"That's my nickname? Prince? I thought it would be Bad boy or something," he says. I shrug.

"I can call you different nicknames," I say. He nods. Suddenly, Mike knocks on the door.

"Come in!" I yell without thinking. He opens the door and once he sees us, his eyes widen.

"What the?" he starts. I stop him though.

"Before you start, no we did not do anything! He is staying with us because his parents are...on a trip! Yes he slept with me! Wait that sounds wrong! No we didn't sleep together we just slept side by side together! We are fully clothed, see! But I swear there is nothing between us! So before this turns into a whole cliché moment where the brother beats up the bad boy just know we did nothing wrong! And he will be staying with us for...a few months. It his choice if he wants to tell you why exactly. Ok you are free to talk, or yell, or beat him up," I say.

"Hey!" Josh says pretending he was hurt. I laugh. Okay maybe I shouldn't have said the whole beating him up part...

"Alisha! Chill I'm not beating him up. I know his home conditions and I don't care if he stays here or sleeps with you! Just don't hurt my sister or I will hurt you and... use protection," he says the last part with a smirk. I look at my brother and then at Josh. Both are smirking.

"And...I'm out!" I say getting out of Josh's grip and running out the door to the kitchen. I hear both of them laugh. I roll my eyes. Boys will be boys right? I sigh and make myself some waffles. the guys come down right when my waffles are done.

"So you made us waffles?" Josh says.

"Um nope. They are all for me!" I say with a smile. There were 4 big waffles. They made their waffles while I get my juice, the syrup and a big bowl of fruit. We all sit down quietly and eat. While I'm eating both of them just stop and stare. I finish chewing and swallowing my mouthful of fruit and waffles.

"Um do I have something on my face?" I ask. They stop staring and Josh speaks.

"No, it's just...you eat...a lot!" he says emphasising the a lot.

"I'm a human. I need to eat! I'm not one of those girls who eats salad everyday for living! I'm a girl who likes food! Now stop judging and staring at me it's really creepy!" I say. They both nod and we all finish our food. Mike gets up and goes to the coffee machine.

"Josh do you want some?" he asks.

"Uh what about me?" I say.

"You just had 4 big waffles, a huge bowl of fruit and a large glass of apple juice. I'm surprised you're not throwing up! You really want coffee?" Mike says.

"Um, I'm still hungry!" I say while getting up. Both boys look at me astonished.

"You're joking right?" Josh says. I shake my head no, and sigh.

"You know what? I will get Starbucks because it's way better than your coffee. Ok well I'm done, you ditching today Josh?" I ask while putting my dishes in the sink. He nods.

"Yeah the guys and I are gonna go over to Zack's," my body stiffens when I hear that name. All the memories, words and actions come rushing back and flooding my head.

"Zack Alexander?" Mike asks. Josh nods.

"Yeah. You know him?" Josh asks.

"Yeah we are like brothers! Can I come too? I want to catch up with him," Mike says.

"Sure," Josh says.

"Hey sis, you wanna come visit Zack? You haven't seen each other in a while," Mike says. I shake my head no.

"Uh, ok well I gotta go get ready!" I say rushing upstairs not daring to look back. I put some clothes on, put my hair into a messy bun, put on some lip gloss and mascara then I run back downstairs with my bag on my shoulder.

"You wanna a lift?" Josh asks. I shake my head no.

"No thanks go enjoy yourself with your...friend. Um take the backyard route," I say.

"What?" Josh asks.

"Um, he used to come over a lot...to hang out with Mike. If you go into the backyard, you will see a gate on the fence. Go through the gate and you will enter his backyard. Just knock and he will open it. Mike knows what I'm talking about. Just follow him," I say and head out the door.

I hop into my car and start the engine. Before you ask, Mike filled up the gas yesterday. I get out of the driveway and ride to school. When I get out I head to Starbucks since I have 20 minutes until school starts. i get my coffee and enter school. This will be a long day.

School was finally done and I was relived. I drive to the mall and park my car. You guessed it! I'm going to the Underworld. I enter and ask Bill, the bartender for a coke. He gives it to me and I head to the punching bag. I punch, kick and let all my anger, frustration, stress and sadness out. Once I was done I go back to my car and drive home. When I enter the house I hear laughter. I go into the living room and see my worst nightmare...Zack Alexander.

"Hey sis! Look who we brought home!" Mike says. I don't say anything I just drop my bag and run upstairs. I shut the door, change into a sports bra ands shorts, put in my headphones and head back downstairs. I wasn't planning on going for a run but I just can't stay here in the same house with him.

"Hold it there Princess, you can at least say hi!" Josh says grabbing my hand so I can't leave. Zack looks at me and smirks.

"Uh h-hey z-Zack," I stutter. He has black hair that was messy. It looked good on him. He was wearing dark jeans and a Nike sweatshirt.

"Hey Alisha. How've you been?" he says inching towards me. I stiffen and try to squirm my way out of Josh's grip.

"What wrong Princess?" he asks. I start getting anxious because Zack was getting closer.

"Nothing, just let go!" I say. Mike comes in and starts to giving me a questioning look.

"What? Where are you going?" Josh says.

"For a run now let go!" I say really wanting to get out of the house.

Zack was now walking towards me. I was getting scared and I knew I would start having a panic attack if I didn't get out of here. Josh still wouldn't let go. I knew I would regret this but I have to. I turn around causing his wrist to twist, but not to bad it would break, twist or get dislocated. Just enough it would hurt him. He lets out a small ow but doesn't let go. Zack was about to touch me but it didn't happen. I flip Josh over my shoulders causing him to fall to the floor. But he was fine just looking at me confused.

As for Zack, well he was about to touch me until I punched him in the stomach and kicked him in the knee. He fell to the ground.

"Alisha! What the hell?" Mike says. That's the last thing I heard before I ran out. Josh and Mike started to run after me and so I started to sprint. I know I'm faster than both of them. I decided not to go to the park because if they did come looking for me, that is the first place they would come to look. Instead I run to a diner I usually went to when I wanted to escape the world.

I enter the dinner and see...Ally? She looks up at me and smiles. I smile back. I go to the booth and sit across from her.

"Al? What are you doing here?" I ask. She shrugs.

"I remember when you, me and Nina used to come here. I wanted to visit it," she says. "What are you doing here?"

I sigh and tell her.

"Zack came over. I went to...the place...and when I got home he was sitting on the couch with Mike and Josh laughing. I ran upstairs changed into well...this, and ran back downstairs. Josh grabbed my hand and after numerous times of asking him to let go, I got fed up and flipped him over. Zack was inching towards me the whole time and when he was about to touch me, well I punched him in the stomach and kicked him in the knee making him fall. I only did that cause I could feel a panic attack rising in me. I ran out the door, Josh and Mike following me, and I sprinted. I got away from them and then I came here," Ally nods.

"I'm sorry Lila," she says. I shake my head.

"It's not your fault. You weren't there so you couldn't help me,"

"No not just because of that. I'm sorry I left you even when I promised I wouldn't," she says sadly. I give her a smile.

"Ally, you didn't completely leave me...ok fine you did. But at least you called and visited when you could! Not like how Nina let Rebecca beat me up," I say. She gasps and I tell her the story,

"Wow, Nina isn't who she was when I left," Ally says sadly. I nod. I look at the time and see it's 8;30. I sigh I have to go home or else the guys will send a search party...wait who am I kidding? I beat 2 of them up! Why would they care about me now...but I still need to go home.

"Ally, I have to go," she nods. We hug each other, say good bye and I head home. When I get home, I look thorough the window outside. I hear and see the TV and decide to go through my window. I know they will ask questions when they realize I'm home. I sigh, climb the tree and open my window. I get inside my room and flop on my bed.

"Stace, how I wish you were here right now. Maybe if you were here, Mom and Dad wouldn't hate me, Nina would still be my friend, Ally would still be here, Zack and I would still be...well I don't know what we were...and everything would just be fine!" I say looking at the ceiling.

I get out my guitar and play a song I've been working on. I am done recording, and I decide to sing a few songs that reflect how I feel. So I press the record button and say:

"October 15, 9:14 p.m. Songs that reflect how I feel." Then I go ahead and sing Rock Me by 1 direction, Miss Movin On by Fifth Harmony and Locked Away by Adam Levine.

"If I got locked away!

And we lost it all today

Tell me honestly,

Would you still love me the same?"

I finish singing Locked Away and sigh.

"Nobody would love me. Nobody does love me or care about me. Thank god I don't let anyone in! I can't imagine what I would do when they leave me! Am I right Stace?" I say.

I know it's weird that I talk to my dead sister, but I know she's listening cause I know she looks over me. I put my guitar away and walk to the door to go to the kitchen. The TV was off so I'm assuming the guys are either out, at Zack's house or in Mike's room. I go downstairs and to my surprise...they are there eating cookies. I freeze when I see them. I slowly back away, hoping they don't see me but...

"Hold it!" they say at the same time. Talk about freaky.

"Where have you been?" Mike says getting out of his chair. I stay silent not wanting to say anything.

"And how did you get in without us seeing you?" Josh says. Still silent.

"And do you want to apologize?" Zack says. I flinch when I hear his voice. The same feeling happens in my stomach just like it did back in freshman year. But it was soon cleared away with fright.

"Answer us!" Mike screams. I feel tears well up in my eyes. He has never screamed at me before.

I still stay silent. Then something I didn't expect to happen...happened. A throbbing pain was left on my cheek...Mike slapped me. I couldn't take it...I ran upstairs and into my room making sure to lock the door cause I could here the guys coming. I went to my closet got some clothes, my tooth brush, my hair brush, my stuff animal, my converse, heels and boots, and some makeup. I was already wearing pyjamas so I didn't bother packing more. I threw the bag out the window, climbed down the tree and got into my car. I drove to one person I could only think of...Nina.

Chapter 13

Alisha's P.O.V

The phone rang. Finally someone picked up.

"Nina?" I ask trying to hold back the tears.

"Yes, who is this?" she says.

"Alisha," I say. She gasps.

"Uh hi," she says.

"I'm coming over," is all I say.

"Uh... o-okay," she stutters. Then I hang up.

After a few minutes I'm parked outside her house. I ring the doorbell and Mrs. Robinson opens up.

"Alisha? Hi dear! Long time no see! How have you been?" she says.

She's in her mid 40's but looks like she is 30. She has dark brown hair and its long. She wore a nightgown and an apron. I smile.

"I'm good! I was wondering could I stay the night?" I ask.

"Of course dear! Oh did you hurt your cheek? It has a bruise," she asks. I touch my cheek and hold back a whimper and force a smile.

"Oh I'm just clumsy! You know me! Is Nina upstairs?" I say.

Mrs. Robinson nods her head. I smile and head upstairs. I knock on the door and Nina says to come in. I enter and we both look at each other not knowing what to say.

"Hey Nina," I say dropping my bag. Her eyes widen when she sees my cheek.

"Oh. My. God. Alisha! Are you ok?" She run up to me and hugs me. I sigh and tell her.

"You remember what happened between me and Zack right?" I ask. She nods.

"Yeah you haven't spoken to each other since the end of freshman year," she says. I nod.

"Well Josh Campbell came over and well he was visiting my brother. They both know Zack so they ditched school to visit him. I came home and he was sitting on the couch with Mike and Josh. I ran upstairs, changed and sort of beat Josh and Zack up in a minor way because they wouldn't let me go outside. Once I beat them up, I went on a run, I came home and came in through my widow. After a few hours I came downstairs and they were waiting for me. They started asking questions and then... Mike slapped me," she gasps. I nod sadly,

"And now you're here," she says. I nod again.

"I hope it's ok I stay the night," I say. She smiles and nods.

"Yeah, I've missed you," she says. I give her a slight smile.

"But this doesn't mean I forgive you," I say. Her smile fades and she nods. I know she knows that I can't forgive her.

"Can we just go to bed? I'm tired after the events of today," I say. She nods and we go to bed.

The next morning, we wake up and get ready for school. I told her family thank you for letting me stay and they said I was welcomed anytime. Then Nina called me over.

"Alisha, I know you can't forgive me that easily but I want you know I'm sorry. I shouldn't have left you. And to make it up to you, I will make sure Rebecca doesn't bug you anymore," she says. I smile at her and hug her. She was shocked for a second but hugs me back.

"Thanks Nina. For this and everything," I say. She smiles back at me. Then I leave.

I get to school and try my best to avoid my brother and Josh. Zack goes to a different school so I didn't have to deal with him, and by the way he is in the same grade as me and Josh.

It was the end of the day and I was exhausted. I drove home and when I parked my car I felt fear overwhelm me. I was not in the mood to climb the tree, but I had too, to enter my room since it was still locked. Unless the guys busted it open, but I doubt it.

I climb the tree and enter the room. Luckily the guys didn't bust it open. I unlock it and go downstairs for food since I only had coffee from Starbucks today. I get downstairs and see Mike on the couch watching TV with the guys. Great! I take a breath and head into the kitchen. I get a plate, two pieces of bread and Nutella. If you didn't know this, Nutella is my life... after Starbucks of course. Then I get some ice from the freezer for my cheek that has been hurting for the whole day. I hear foot steps and sigh. I have to face them sooner or later tight?

"Alisha?" I hear Mike say. I flinch and freeze. Okay I know I said I have to face them sooner or later but now I choose later rather than sooner! I awkwardly turn my body with the ice on my cheek. His face was soft and full of regret. I relax my body until I see Zack behind Mike. I go stiff again and my body starts to shake. All three guys walk towards me. I try to move back but the counter was keeping me back.

"Before you guys beat me up can I at least write a will or something? Or say goodbye to Ally?" I say with fear in my voice. They look at each other and chuckle a little. Oh no this is the end of me. And Mike out of all people will be my murderer? And I trusted Josh. Ok I didn't completely trust him, but i didn't think he would be part of a gang that kills me! And Zack...well I can suspect something like that from him.

"Alisha we aren't gonna kill you," Josh says. Even though I was relieved, my body was on high alert that the slightest movement will make me flinch. My heart was racing like crazy! I'm not joking. They were maybe...5 inches away from me. Yes I'm a fighter but I don't think I can face 3 built guys. Oh how I wish The Rippers were here.

"We just want to talk," Zack says stepping closer I flinch and jump onto the counter and sit. They look at me and sigh.

"Alisha what was your little outburst yesterday about?" Mike asks. I look at him confused. Really?! He isn't going to apologize to me?

"Uh don't you have something to say to me first?" I ask with a shocked face. He sighs,

"Look Alisha I'm sorry I slapped you. I didn't mean too. I was just mad and angry. I shouldn't have taken it out on you. It's my fault. I still love you though. I don't know what came over me. I was just, mad and I should have got rid of my anger in a better manner than violence," he says. "Can you try and forgive me?" his eyes were soft, sad and guilty. I give him a small smile and nod. He beams and comes closer to hug me but I flinch. He looks taken back but I quickly open my arms indicating for a hug. He smiles and hugs me. Then he steps back.

"Now back to my question. What came over you yesterday?" Mike says. I shrug.

"I wanted to go on a run and you guys were holding me back. I tried asking you to let go but you wouldn't! You were hurting me and I didn't want to go as far as I did but I was scared and I did what I did," I say. Suddenly, I knew they would ask how I did what I did. So I quickly add in

"And I have no idea how I flipped you or punched or kicked you. I'm sorry," I say. They just look at me and nod.

"Apology accepted!" Zack says with a smirk and coming in for a hug but I flinch. He stops and just backs away. I get off the counter with my food and walkover to the living room and change the channel to Pretty Little Liars. It was the Christmas special in season 5 with Alison. Hanna is my favorite. They guys come in and grunt that they can't watch whatever game they were watching before. They knew I was still jumpy so they made sure they stayed a good distance away. I kept on gasping and screaming at the characters in the show. The guys kept telling me to shut up but of course I ignored them.

I get up to put my dishes away since it was commercial. Suddenly, I feel hands wrap around my waist and jump and turn around to see...Zack.

"I don't know why you are so jumpy around me but it's getting old. I'm back and here to stay, you better start talking to me or else things will get ugly. Do I need to remind you what happened back in freshman year when you ignored me?" he says. Memories flooded my mind again. I shake my head no while looking down.

"Good, well lets go back and watch your show," he says like nothing happened.

I was shaking but I was able to walk back to the living room. I sat down but every so often I would glance over at Zack. He wasn't even watching the show, he was watching me. When Pretty Little Liars was over, I run upstairs. I get into my pyjamas and head to bed. I hear my door open and I glance over to see Josh taking of is shirt and pants and hop into bed. He wraps his arms around me and for some reason I feel safe, like no one can touch me. I sigh and let my dreams take over my body.

"Hey Zack!" I go to hug him but he pushes away.

"Alisha," he says uneasy.

"Is everything alright? We are gonna be late if we don't get going now! You know how Nina gets when we show up late," I say urging him out the door.

"No, this can't wait," he says inching towards me. Oh My God! Is this really happening? Does he really like me like that? Does he feel the same way as I do? He has been my crush for...7 years! This is actually happening!

"I know you like me, but unfortunately for you, I don't feel the same way. You aren't my type. You aren't pretty, you're pretty ugly. You're fat. I'm surprised you can't see that yourself. And most of all, you're a pain. I don't know how I've put up with you for 9 years. Yes we were best friends but not anymore. Sorry sweetie but this friendship is done. Don't expect me to change my mind and come running back like those cliché books you read. Goodbye Alisha, you might want to change if you ever want a guy to look at you in a good way, because the way they look at you now, you might as well move to the North Pole, you and Santa Clause will make a beautiful couple, if he can even tolerate you because I sure can't anymore. See you never." He says coldly.

I was shocked, I couldn't move. I was frozen. But I could sure speak.

"How can you do this to me? Why? What did I ever do to you? You said you wouldn't leave me! You promised Zack!" I cry. He smirks.

"I just can't deal with your crap anymore. It's just not worth it! And I don't care that I promised something in the first grade!" He responds coldly.

"No! Please Zack! Don't do this! I don't know what has gotten into you, but this isn't you!" I cry while grabbing onto his hand trying not to let him leave. Then he punches me. He punches me in the face, stomach, waist and jaw. I fell to the ground and forced myself not to cry. He kicked me multiple times but I stayed strong. Once he was done abusing me he kneels down so I can hear him.

"I know you want to cry. And I know why you aren't going too. Now suck it up sweetie and wait till the next time I see you. I'm gonna beat you up so bad even if you didn't even mean to cross paths with me. And you better not ignore me or else I will hunt you down myself. You are my little toy and punching bag now! Goodbye!" he says and walks out the door leaving me helpless.

I tried ignoring him but every time I would go out he would drag me into an alley and beat me up because I was his toy. I finally told his parents and they sent him away to a place in the summer to get his act together. After that, it was like we never knew each other. But the nightmares kept coming back to me and now every time he comes near me, I flinch and get scared.

Chapter 14

Alisha P.O.V

I wake up screaming, not crying, just a few tears. Josh was looking at me worried. I looked at the clock 5:45 a.m. Might was well take an extra long shower. I jump out of bed, ignoring Josh's questions and hop into the shower. When I get out I put on some high wasted shorts, a pink muscle tee that has a heart in the middle and my ankle boots. I dry my hair, curl it, put some red lipstick and mascara then run out the door without breakfast. I hear all the guys scream after me but I ignore them. Josh probably told them. Since it's still pretty early I decided to walk instead of drive. I get to school and cross the street to Starbucks and get my Pumpkin Spice Latte. Heaven!!!!

I walk back to school and head to my classes. The school day passed on and Josh wasn't at school. I walk home until I stop because somebody turns me around. I'm in front of Zack Alexander.

"Hello Alisha," he says with a smirk.

"Hi," I say looking at the ground.

"So I have some great news!" he says like a girl.

"You're moving to Alaska?" I snap at him and suddenly regret it. He looks at me but pretends that I didn't say anything.

"No. Guess who's moving to your school?" he says pointing to himself. My mouth falls open. No! This can't be happening!

"Don't look so surprised sweetie. Anyways, I need someone to give me a tour of the school," he says inching towards, I step back.

"Find someone else and not me," I say trying to escape.

"Come on babe, you know you still like me, and I know you want me," he whispers into my ear. I back away again.

"No! Just no! Stay away from me!" I say trying to walk away but he stops me.

"Ok fine. But just so you know, we will be the hot new couple! I can almost guarantee it!" he says with a smirk. I look at him with an astonished face.

"As if! Did you forget what you said to me back at the end of freshman year?" I say.

"No! But I know you still like me and just like in the stupid books you read, the good girl and bad boy always end up together," he says.

"Not that I'm saying we will be a couple but, you are not the bad boy of this school. Josh is," I say with a grin.

"So you and him will be a thing?" he says.

"No, I'm just making it clear to you that you are not the bad boy and we will not be a couple," I say.

"Oh. Well I'm gonna make this clear to you that Josh has some competition of being the number one bad boy in this school," he says with a snarl.

"Ok fine that's none of my business. But you and me will never be a couple and nor will me and Josh!" I say in his face.

"Oh sweetie! You should follow those cliché books you read! Because again, the good girl and bad boy always end up hooking up!" he says.

"Well because of you and some other people, I don't believe in clichés, fairy tales, trust and especially love! So back off Zack! You may be in my school but that doesn't mean I will talk to you so don't waist your breath!" I snarl at him.

He pushes me against the tree leaving my back throbbing. Then he punches my side. I fall to the ground and he kicks my side, in the same spot he punched it. I scream in pain and he covers my mouth. I feel exactly how I felt back in freshman year.

"Shhhh baby doll! No you will talk to me unless you want this to happen again. And I hate hurting you!" he says kneeling down and whispering it in my ear. I shiver. "Goodbye for now," he says and walks away leaving me there like he did 2 years ago in my house. I get up and walk home, pain shooting through my side like a thousand punches were being thrown at me with each step I take. I enter house and walk upstairs not bothering saying hi to the guys. I slam my door shut and ice my side.

I put on some comfy clothes. Sweat pants, a t-shirt and I put my hair into a messy bun. I flop on my bed and just look at the ceiling.

"Stacey, I wish you were here because my life is so screwed up!" I say and sigh.

I decided to finish my homework. By the time I was done it was 9 o'clock. I walk downstairs to get some juice with my phone in my hand checking social media. I get some juice and my phone rings.

"Hello?" I say.

"Hey Alisha it's Ally," Ally says.

"Hey Ally! What's up?" I say.

"Nothing just wanted to talk. You ok?" she says. I sigh.

"Sort of. Guess who's transferring into my school?" I say.

"Who?" She says.

"Zack," I say.

"Oh my! Will you be okay?"

"Yeah I guess. What can I do? I can't exactly tell him to go away. I mean yeah he will torture me and you know what I mean by that, but I'm a tough cookie," I say while sitting on the counter.

"Lila, I know you aren't ok. I can hear it in your voice and when I see you I can see it in your eyes, your heart is breaking!" Ally says. I sigh.

"Al, my heart is already broken! Everybody I ever let in broke a piece of it! Yes I go to school with no friends but I'm ok with that! I mean I can't blame anyone! I'm ugly, fat and no guy wants to look at me...HE was right all those years ago," I say. She sighs and I can hear it in her voice that she is sad.

"Alisha! You're not ugly or fat! You're beautiful! I wish I was there to help you, I know your life is hard," she says.

"Yes my life is hard because everyone I ever trusted has let me down...you know except for Mike, and you in a way. But others lives are worst! I cant keep on being sad for myself," I say.

"Yeah but you're literally breaking cause you aren't letting anyone in!" she cries. I sob trying to hold back the tears yet some fall out. NO! I will not cry over myself. That's pathetic.

"Fine! Yes you're right! I am breaking slowly! And you know why? Because everyone I ever trusted and everyone who said they wouldn't leave me has left me! The Rippers left me to go to Paris. Stacey left me when I was 5! 5! Because she was killed and I could have down something about it! I could have stayed awake and maybe just maybe told Bob to kill me instead of her! Nina left me for the popular crowd! My parents left me because they blame me for Stacey's death and I still do! Zack left me for God knows why! YOU left me stranded because you had to move! Now Mike will leave me next year for college! He says he won't leave me but when it comes down to me and his dream he will pick his dream in a heartbeat! I will not let him miss out on college because of me Ally! I won't! I will keep this act together until he leaves! Then! Then I don't know what will become of me! The only people behind the walls I put up are you and Mike! Josh...I don't know about him, but I swear I am a complete and utter mess!" I cry.

This time the tears come flowing out. I needed to get everything out. Each tear was for a different reason. One for Ally, one for Nina, one for Stacey, one for my parents, one for Mike, one for Josh, one for Zack, one for the Rippers, basically anyone who has left me or will leave me. I can't believe now is the time I let the waterworks come out. On the other end I could here Ally sob.

"I am so sorry Alisha. You don't deserve this," she says with a soft tone.

"Maybe I do Al. Maybe life is punishing me for letting my sister die when I could have saved her," I say with a soft tone.

"No. You were 5. You couldn't have done anything." Ally says with a stern voice. I sigh.

"Thanks for listening to me Ally, I miss you so much," I say still crying.

"I miss you too Alisha. But tell me one thing...are you mad that I left? Answer truly," she says.

"Yes I am mad that you left. I am mad at everyone who left me, even Stacey. But in the end, they all left me for a reason. Some because they had no choice, like you and Stacey. Others because they were sick of me like Him, Nina and my parents," I say.

"Well I'm sorry. Please forgive me," she says with guilt in her voice.

"I do Al, I do. And I will be fine, I gotta go. Love ya," I say.

"Love you too Alisha, I will visit you soon," she says. I smile and hang up. I sigh, I hope the guys didn't hear any of that. I walk upstairs into my room and head to bed. Josh will come when he's tired...

Josh's P.O.V

We heard her whole conversation. Me, Mike and Zack. At first we were spying on her looking for the perfect moment to scare her, for fun. Until we heard her conversation. It was heartbreaking. Ok I know I sound like a girl but I don't care. So many people have left her. Heck her own parents left her! No wonder she has insecurity issues. And then she says she's ugly and fat when she isn't! When I find the guy who said that to her I will kill him.

After I heard her say Zack left her I turned to him. He didn't look shocked or sad. He literally just stood there emotionless. I was completely confused. Mike was sad that she felt that way and now he knows that she will be a mess once he leaves for college. Now he is even planning not to go!

But what really shocked me is when I heard her crying her eyes out. She sounded so lost and hurt. I wanted to run up to her and comfort her but I knew that was a bad idea. She finally let all the tears out after 6 years. That is amazing. She ran upstairs and went to bed. The guys and I talked and we agreed to tell her in the morning that we heard her. She has the right to know. She wasn't going to school tomorrow because of her breakdown today, we are taking her out tomorrow instead, to take her mind of things.

I open her bedroom door and just stared at her. She looks so innocent. There were tear stains on her face and still tears rolling down her cheek. She was breaking. And that isn't a metaphor in this case. Our plan in the morning is for us to tell her that we heard her. After that, we would take her to a place to take her mind of things and hope that she will be alright. I get into the bed and wrap my arms around her. She shifts around a little but didn't move my hand. I bring her closer to me. All I want at this point is to make sure she is safe. But the one thing that is going through my mind that I keep noticing is why she is so jumpy whenever Zack is around. Whenever he talks or walks up to her she flinches or jumps like he will hurt her. And I'm going to figure out why...

Authors Note

Hey guys! Hope you like the book so far! Sorry I haven't been updating. I've been updating a lot on my new story Good Girl Gone Bad. It's going to be a series so please go read that! And of course please rate and comment because I really do appreciate it! Thanks bye and love you!!

Chapter 15

Zack's P.O.V

After we heard her conversation we quietly went upstairs because we didn't want her knowing we heard her. Mike and Josh were completely shocked. I was shocked but not as much. Especially all that stuff she said about me. I knew when she said him she was referring to me. Can't blame her! But that doesn't mean I won't stop torturing her. Yes I feel kind of guilty but not as much as I should. I don't care about her anymore. Yes I don't like hurting her but she just gets me so fed up when she ignores me or stands up to me! I don't know where she gets the confidence from but she has a bolt load of it!

We were best friends for 9 years. But throughout grade 8-9 I just got fed up with her! Not so much Nina and Ally just Alisha! And when I found out she had a crush on me I got disgusted I mean why would I go out with a girl like Alisha? A goodie two shoes, a nerd! An ugly person! Yuck! I still gag. I know that's harsh but I still don't care about her life or her feelings. However she has changed. I mean she looks a little cuter now...

When we were done discussing the plan, I went downstairs to sleep on the couch. I don't get why they are doing this for her. She's not special! She's just like every other girl I know! Wanting attention! Unfortunately she's getting a lot of it.

Alisha's P.O.V

I wake up the next morning on my own. I look at my phone and realize it's...10 o'clock?! I'm so late for school! I get up pretty easy today because their wasn't a hand wrapped around me...what? My head whips around when I hear my bathroom door open. There I see Josh, in a towel. Nothing but a towel.

"Oh dear god! My innocent eyes!" I say closing my eyes and putting my hand out to cover them. Ok cliché I know and I suppose I'm exaggerating a bit but I don't care! I didn't need to see that!

"Oh come on Princess! Stop being a drama queen !" He says with a laugh.

"I've always been a drama queen moron! Deal with it!" I say still closing my eyes. "Now go in the bathroom and put some clothes on!"

"I'd rather change in front of you!" He says. I freeze. Holy rutabagas no!

"No way Campbell in the bathroom now!" I scream. He chuckles and goes into the bathroom. I spring out of bed and quickly change before he gets out. A skirt and a crop top. Plain and simple yet cute. I put on my ankle boots and rush out the door. I'm about the open the door when a hand grabs mine.

"Where are you going?" Zack says. Oh no! He has my hand. I flinch and turn around.

"I-I am g-going to s-school," I stutter. He chuckles.

"Not today sweetheart," he says. I look at him with a questioning look. Mike and Josh come in at that moment.

"He's right sis. We gotta talk," Mike says. I give them another questioning look and sigh. Ok then? This is weird. We all sit down at the table. The three of them across from me. I sit there uncomfortably because they stare at me. I avoid eye contact.

Mike sighs and says

"We heard you,"

I look at him with a confused expression. In my head I'm hoping and praying it's not what I think.

"Your conversation with Ally yesterday, we heard you," Mike adds on. My mouth opens.

"Oh that? Ha ha ha I was joking! Ha ha ha!" I laugh nervously hoping they'd buy it.

"Quit the act we know you're lying," Josh says. I stop. Um...well...I don't know what I'm suppose to do.

"Is that really how you feel?" Mike says. I don't say a word.

"We understand you don't let anyone in! But you have to start! And who the heck are the Rippers?" Mike adds. I still don't say anything, I just play with my fingers.

"Alisha! Say something! We know you're breaking! Every time we look in your eyes all we see is sadness, anger, guilt and fear! You have to talk to someone! Let someone in!" Josh exclaims. I look at him. Then at Mike, then at Zack who has been silent.

"Dude say something!" Josh says to Zack. Zack looks up at me.

"You gotta stop being afraid of people!" He says. I jump up from my chair making it fall back.

"Stop being afraid of people? Really Zack? Out of all people I didn't expect those words to come out of your mouth! If you heard my conversation yesterday then you know why I'm scared of people! I can't trust anybody! Everyone who has ever stepped foot in my life has left or will leave! All of you will! It's karma! Zack you already have! I don't know why you came back but from the looks of it and how you treat me, I want you out! I don't need anybody! Who cares if I'm breaking? Nobody has noticed till now! I'm fine! I'm strong! I have people in my life but one way or another they leave! That's just the story of my life! If you leave and come back I can't trust you! I can't trust anyone! Especially you Zack Alexander! You hurt me the most!" I cry. Tears roll down my cheek. Each word is filled with even more hatred towards Zack. All 3 boys are just left stunned.

"What the hell is she talking about Zack?" My brother says turning his attention to Zack. He stays quiet.

"Yes Zack what am I talking about? Why so silent? You don't have any comebacks or comments or words today? Why? You had so many yesterday! And maybe a few actions too! In lighten them best friend! Cause I'm sick of having to cover for you!" I scream at him and run upstairs with that. I slam my door and cry my pillow. Why do I have so many tears? I thought I got rid of all of them yesterday! Guess not. I sigh and play my guitar. I was singing and playing Boom Clap by Charli XCX.

Mike's P.O.V

"Zack what's going on?" I say. He sighs and tells us everything.

"I got sick and tired of your stupid sister throughout 8th and 9th grade. So one day in the summer I told her and maybe threw in some violence. After that, whenever I saw her I would beat her up. Even if I didn't see her I would come over and beat her up cause I was mad that she was ignoring me. My parents sent me away to get help. When I came back I ignored her for 2 years. Then you guys came over and we'll we are here," he says. I was left there stunned. My best friend, of who knows how long, beat up my sister! More than once!

"I'm not gonna fight you because that would make me just as bad as you. But I will say something to you. You aren't my best friend. This you isn't the real you-" he cuts me off.

"You sound exactly like your sister!" Zack laughs. I sigh and continue.

"You betrayed me and your other best friend. We can't ever forgive you. You knew she didn't let anyone in easily yet she let you in. You just broke the most trust someone will ever give you in your life. I hope you're happy, you can go now," I say pointing towards the door. "And don't touch my sister again," I add in.

"You might not want to kill him, but I sure as hell do!" Josh says. He launches towards Zack and throws a punch. He goes for another but I hold him back.

"Let me at him! Let me at him!" He says.

"He's not worth the energy," I say. Josh calms down and lets Zack go with a black eye.

"I can't believe he did that. I can't believe Alisha never told me!" I scream with my head in my hands.

"Don't beat yourself up about it. The best thing we could do now is be there for your sister. And now the mystery is closed for me so I don't have to go all Sherlock Homes," Josh says. I look at him with a confused face.

"I noticed how every time Zack touched or talked to Alisha she would flinch or jump, like he was gonna hurt her. I guess now we know why," Josh says. I nod.

"Let's go see how you're sister is doing," he adds on. I don't say anything, I just get up and walk upstairs, Josh behind me. We knock on Alisha's door with no answer. I knock again and still no answer. All we hear is crying. I open the door and I don't see Alisha but I hear crying and screaming coming from her bathroom. We run inside and see her cutting a deep cut with a blade into her side. Josh runs to her and takes the blade away from her hand. I stood there shocked. I literally just watched my 16 year old sister cut herself. Oh my god. The worst part was, she was gonna need stitches.

Alisha falls to the ground crying. Both me and Josh sit on each side comforting her. This was all Zack's fault.

"It's ok Alisha, don't worry. You're safe now. He won't get to you I promise," Josh cooed while she cried into his chest. I take some rubbing alcohol and wipe her side, cleaning of all the blood. I knew how to stitch up wounds since I want to be a doctor so I get up and get a needle and thread.

"Lila you need stitches," I say coming back into the bathroom where Alisha was sitting. She stopped crying and was now sniffling.

"O-okay," she stutters. Her eyes were puffy and red and there were tear stains on her face. She was a mess.

Josh starts to get up but she grabs his hand. "Please, st-stay," she says. He sits down while she buries her head into his shirt. I stitch up her cut while she flinches every so often. When I was done, Josh picked her up and set her on her bed where she fell asleep. We walk out of her room and into the kitchen.

"I can't believe I just saw that," I say while sitting down on one end of the couch. Josh comes and sits on the other end.

"I know bro, but all we can do now is be there for her," he says while looking for the remote for the TV. I find it and pass it to him.

"Yeah, I guess, now she really needs some friends," I say.

"Well she has 7 right now," Josh says, and turns on the TV and flipping through channels.

"What?" I ask him.

"You, me, Ally, Luca, Jace, Chad, and Dylan," Josh responds and settles on a soccer game.

"Oh right, yeah now we just have to be there for her," I say. Josh sighs and nods. We get comfortable and watch the soccer game silently.

Chapter 16

Alisha's P.O.V

I wake up peacefully and yawn. I sit up in bed and sigh. I remember everything that happened. The words I said to Zack, the blade, my side, the stitches, everything. My side doesn't hurt at all. I mean it hurt but I felt satisfied.

I look at my phone and see it's 1 o'clock. I slept for a good 2 hours. Great! I get out of bed and throw on some sweat pants, and a plain black tank top. I put my hair in a high ponytail and pack my bag. Deodorant, a sweater, water bottle, my cell phone and ear plugs. I throw my bag out the window and climb down the tree. I decided to run instead of taking my car. It will warm up my body for todays fight. Yes I'm going to fight today. Not punch a punching bag, fight a person. I walk into the Underworld and everybody turns to look at me. I smirk and walk over to Jack, the announcer.

"Yo, Jack! I want to fight today!" I say to him. Jack grins at me.

"Lucky for you kiddo I have the perfect opponent for you," Jack says and announces the fight.

"And today! We have Dynamite facing Skull!" He screams into the microphone. The crowd cheers for me and only some for Skull. I get into the my fighting position and watch my opponent carefully. Skull was built. Like really built!

He was left handed and always kept his weight on his left leg. He swung a punch at my stomach but I dodged it. The crowd cheers. Ok so his strongest feature is a punch. I kick my leg into his left leg making him fall. Yes! But I guess he wasn't going to give up that easily. He unexpectedly got up at kicked my side. I fell to the ground. That really hurt! But I wasn't going to give up. I never lose a match. I get up and whip my hair at his face which scratches his cheek and than I punch his stomach. He jumps back and holds his cheek. He punches my side, in the exact spot he kicked it in. I kick his left knee then his right making him fall to the ground. I put one foot on his stomach and raise my hands in victory! The crowd goes wild!

My special move is my hair whip. Since my hair is thick, I use it to my advantage. I always put my hair in a ponytail and when things are getting ugly for me I whip it at their face. The ends of my hair are sharp and pointy. I don't know why, but I'm glad they are! I get my things and head out with my head held high. But my side was killing me. I don't know how I survived that but I did. I think some of my ribs were broken or at least bruised. I limp back and head in through the front door of my house. Josh and Mike run to the door and sigh in relief.

"We were scared to death about you! Where did you go?" Mike says.

"The mall," I say with a shrug. I try to walk as normally as possible so they don't suspect anything.

"Ok but you have to tell us!" Mike cries.

"I know and I'm sorry! Next time I will tell you I just didn't think you would let me because of the incident earlier today," I say and almost whisper the last part.

"Yeah, and speaking of that, we need to talk about that. Zack is gone so we don't need to worry about him. And he told us everything," Josh says. I nod.

"Ok well lets talk," I say walking to the couch and plopping myself on it.

"Why? When?" Mike says. I sigh.

"It all started the day when Zack came back into the house. You know when I beat him and Josh up, sorry about that again," I say.

"Over it," Josh says with a small smile.

"I cut a small cut on my wrist, it felt satisfying. I didn't want to do it again but each time he was here I did more and more of it. Especially when he beat me up after school. I got fed up and did it. I know it's bad and I'm gonna stop I promise," I say. They both nod their heads.

"We are so sorry you had to live your life with so much hurt, and pain. Not to mention friendless," Mike says. I shrug.

"I'm ok. I mean that's just my life," I say. They shake their heads no.

"Well you have 7 friends now. Me, the guys, Ally and Mike," Josh says. I smile I actually have true friends? Ok I will let them in behind the walls. Lets see what happens.

"Thanks," I say and I go up and hug him. He hugs me back and then I go and hug Mike.

"But Josh, why do you care so much? I get Mike because he's my brother but you, you barely know me," I say. Josh shrugs.

"I just do. I mean you helped me by giving me a place to stay! The least I can do is be your friend and help you get through high school in one piece," he says with humour in his voice, I smile and giggle.

"Well thanks, oh and I need the TV," I say.

"No way the game is going on!" Mike whines like a child. I roll my eyes and shake my head.

"Boo hoo for you. Scream Queens is on I need to know what's going to happen to Grace and the Red Devil and who the baby in the bath tub was!" I cry. Both guys were so lost.

"Devil? What? Is he like the son of Satan or something?" Josh says. I laugh and quickly grab the remote from the coffee table before either of them can flinch. They grunt and I laugh and flip to Scream Queens.

After an hour of wonderful Scream Queens, I get hungry so I order pizza from Pizza Hut. Only the best in my opinion. The pizza man delivers the pizza 45 minutes later and by now I could eat a house! I gobbled up 4 big slices of cheesy goodness. This time the boys minded their own business and didn't stare at me like they were stalkers. Yet I could see them looking at me every so often. When I was done I put my dishes away and headed upstairs Josh following behind me. I didn't want to get up late tomorrow so I wanted to sleep early. I changed into my pyjamas in the bathroom and hopped into bed beside Josh. I forgot he always wrapped his arm around me and once he did I flinch and whimper a little. I turn to face him and he looks confused.

"Did I hurt you," he asks.

"What no!" I say nervously.

"Princess...what's wrong?" Josh says in a concern voice.

"Nothing!" I say still nervous. He still didn't look convinced, he wraps his arm around me again and tries to bring me in closer. He was pushing down on my side. Even though it was just a little, it hurt. I whimpered again but a little louder. Suddenly, Josh pulls my shirt up and see's my bruise. Uh oh!

"Oh my god Alisha! What the hel-heck happened?" he screams.

"It's nothing! Just a little bruise..." I say while trying to avoid eye contact.

"A little bruise? I think some of your ribs are shifted or broken!" he says. I don't say anything. "Ok this is my turn to help you, this will hurt. A lot. Hold on to my chest cause I know who will want to dig your nails into something and I would rather it be me than you," he says. I nod my head and do what I'm instructed to do.

'Ok...1,2,3," he says and I feel my ribs move. I cry and dig my nails into his skin. He does that three more times and I swear he has scars from my nails.

"All done, but there is still a big bruise," Josh says. I nod. I didn't even realize I was crying until Josh wiped away a tear.

"Thanks," I say. He smiles and we head off to bed. Please oh please don't let me have a nightmare!

Chapter 17

Alisha's P.O.V

The next morning we woke up and got ready for school. Josh said he would take me instead of driving my own car. I went along with it because I was tired since I had a nightmare. It was about me and Zack. Shocker! Not!

~Nightmare~

"Hey Ughlisha!" Zack says.

I don't say anything. I just ignore him like I always do. Why does he bug me so much?

"So where are we going today? Woods? Alley? Cave? I decided it was only fair to give you the option today on where to beat you up," he says.

How considerate of him! Jerk.

"Are you gonna ignore me?" He asks. I could hear the anger in his voice.

No sheez Sherlock!

"You know what I'm capable of," he says grabbing my arm. I get whipped around and turned to face him.

"Let go!" I say through gritted teeth.

"Oh so now you talk?" He says with a smirk.

"Let go!" I say again.

"No!" He says.

On instinct I kick him in the shin and then punch him in the jaw. When he lets go of my other hand I punch him in the stomach and then kick him in the stomach too.

"Oh so you're fighting back now are you?" He says. I stay silent.

What did I just do? Now he knows my secret. No! Please no!

"Silent again? Well, we'll see about that," he says and lunges towards me.

~End of nightmare~

I shot up after that and was breathing heavily.

When we were downstairs, we skipped breakfast and went straight for Starbucks. I got a Pumpkin Spice Latte. Then we headed back to school.

"So you wanna tell me about your nightmare?" Josh ask.

"What?" I say.

"Don't play dumb with me, I know you had a nightmare last night," Josh says. "So what was it?" He say and stops in his tracks.

"Uh would you believe it was on the end of the world?" I ask.

"Nope. Not for a second," he says. I sigh.

"It was about Zack," I say.

"Someone talking about me? I knew you still liked me," Zack says from behind me.

I jump and turn around. Josh comes in front of me and glares at Zack. I don't see him glaring but I know he is. I peek from behind him and Zack catches my stare.

"Get away from her," Josh says. At this point we got a crowd. I knew at any second now people would start changing "Fight! Fight! Fight!" So I had to get them away from each other.

"Why? We are best friends," Zack says. That ticked me off.

"Pshh best friends? Oh no! We lost that a long time ago when you beat me up in my house! And then left me there after calling me fat, ugly and other words that I shouldn't use! So don't think I can ever call you my best friend again. You are not the boy who was my best friend. Nor the guy I liked. No. You are a monster," I snarl and walk away.

I heard "oohs" and "you just got served" and "burn" from behind me and I felt satisfied. I heard footsteps coming from behind me. Probably Josh. But I was wrong. It was Zack. He turns me around and puts his hands on my shoulders and shoves me. I put one of my hands on his and flip him. He falls to the ground and groans.

"Oh did that hurt? Good. Now leave me alone!" I scream and run away. I heard foot steps coming from behind me and I thought it was Zacks. I kept running and started crying because I was getting scared. I was losing breath and I couldn't stop crying. I ended up getting and anxiety attack and falling to the floor.

"Shh princess it's ok. It's just me" Josh says. I got a flashback of me and Zack.

~Flashback~

People were bullying me. They hurt me. They cut me with scissors on my cheek. I ran. I ran far. I heard footsteps behind me and I thought it was them. So I cried while I ran. I ran a mile and I still heard the foot steps. I was still crying.

"Please go away!" I screamed while still running and looking forward.

I could still hear the footsteps and I was still running. It's sort of amazing how a 5th grader can run so far and still keep going. But I was getting tired. And I was still crying and screaming. So I fell against a tree and cried into my knees.

"Alisha, it's ok. It's just me," Zack says.

I look into his dreamy eyes. Maybe one day we will be together. I hope so. But I'm glad he's my best friend. And he always will be.

"Will we be best friends forever?" I sniffle.

"I thought we were?" He says.

"No we are best friends," I respond.

"I'm sure we will be. Now and forever. No matter what," he says. I smile.

"Promise?" I ask.

"I promise Lila. I promise," he says. I smile wider and hug him. He hugs me back and we got up and walked back to school.

~End of Flashback~

"Hey are you ok?" Josh asks.

"Hmm? Oh yeah I'm fine just thought of something," I sniffle.

"Ok," he says.

"Are we friends?" I ask randomly.

"Of course! And at this point I think I'm your best friend forever," he says with a grin.

"You can't," I say.

"What?" He asks.

"You can't be my best friend forever. If you do, then you will end up like him. Leaving me," I say.

"I don't follow," Josh says.

"In 5th grade! He promised we'd be best friends forever. Now and forever! Forever never lasts! It's just a word someone made for lost hope. Forever is what broke our friendship. I can't lose yours" I say.

"Oh alright. Then I guess I'm your very, very, very, close friend," Josh says.

"I guess so," I say.

The bell rings after that and we get up. Josh walks me to my first class and says we will meet up at 2nd period aka Chemistry. Ironic huh? I walk in and see everyone staring at me.

"What?!" I ask a little loudly.

"You're Alisha! You beat up new kid!" A nerd says. I roll my eyes.

"Yes because new kid was my friend. Was is the key word here. He was being rude to me and abusing me so I beat him up!" I say and walk to my seat.

A jock was sitting there and once he saw me he shot up and ran to the back. I smirk. The football jocks are scared of me! This could be good. Suddenly everyone gasps. I turn around and see Zack. He had and ice pack at the back of his head. Oops.

"It's new kid! And Alisha! In the same class!" The same nerd says. I think his name was Stewart.

"New kid has a name nerd! Zack. Now shut up and stop staring!" Zack screams at Stewart and walks to the seat behind me. Oh goodie! Note the sarcasm.

The teacher walks in shortly after and introduces Zack. You know the normal new kid routine. He goes back to his seat and I could feel him sending me death daggers.

"Ok class! Here is your project! I want you to pair up with someone in the class that you aren't on good terms with. Find out why, you aren't on good terms, then write a report on the real them. This is due in one month," The teacher says.

I look around and the only person I had bad terms with is....Zack. Nuts!

"Damn we're partners," I mumble under my breath.

"I guess we are," Zack says.

I turn to face him. And I could see all the rage in his eyes.

"My house. After school," I say. And with that the bell rings.

I gather my stuff and walk to Chemistry. Oh god this is gonna be a long month.

--------------Authors Note

Bam! Another chapter! I hope you liked it! Did ya? Well if you did Vote and Comment please! And yes I know drama! A lot will be discovered in the next few chapters. And maybe, just maybe, Zack you'll learn about

Alisha's secret! Then what? And maybe you'll discover the real reason Zack left Alisha. What? You don't think there's more to the story. Oh but there is! Stay tuned and in the mean time read my other story Good Girl Gone Bad! Bye bye and love you guys! Thank you for the support!

Chapter 18

Alisha's P.O.V

School passed by in a blur and before I knew it I was walking to my car at the end of the day. I didn't really want to go home but if I didn't then Zack would probably get beaten up by Josh and Mike. So I'd better go. Not that I cared!

I pulled up in my driveway and walked to the door. I unlocked it and ran upstairs to change. Sweat pants and a plain tank top. My hair was thrown into a high ponytail and I ran back downstairs to eat.

I got some cookies from the fridge and put them in the oven to bake. 10 minutes later they were done. Yay! I heard a knock on the door and I went to go open it.

I opened it and there stood Zack. I let him in and he went to the kitchen.

"What's this?" he asks while pointing to the cookies.

"Um my cookies?" I say with a duh tone.

"Yeah I know but aren't they for me too?" he asks.

"Pshh no!" I say.

Suddenly a flashback comes to mind. When Bob killed Stacey because she didn't make cookies for him. Zack came closer and I backed up.

Wait! Isn't the oven still hot? Oh my god.

"Zack! Please don't kill me like he did to her! Please! I will make you some damn cookies just please!" I plead.

"Woah! I'm not gonna kill you! Chill! I just wanted milk and you're standing right in front of the fridge!" he says.

It took me a minute to process it and then I looked back. I was standing in front of the fridge.

"Oops," I say and shift to the side. "My bad," I add in.

"Whatever," he says and gets some milk.

The door opens and reveals Josh and Mike laughing. They come into the kitchen and see Zack. They look like lions ready to kill.

"Woah! Chill tigers! He's just here for a project we have to do! Chill!" I say.

"He didn't hurt you right?" Mike says still watching Zack.

"No! Now go!" I say and shoo them away.

"Fine, but, if there is any trouble-" Josh starts but I cut him off.

"Yeah yeah I call my knight and shinning armors now go!" I exclaim. They surrender and head upstairs.

"Sorry," I mumble and head into the living room. Zack followed.

"Yeah ok. Anyways, I guess we might as well get to know one another," Zack says.

"Really? Zack I know we aren't on best terms but we were still best friends. Tell me if I'm wrong. You're favorite colour is red, your favorite sport is soccer, you hate school but you do your work so you can get away from this place, you have 1 brother, your parents are still together, you hate when people aren't intimidated by you, your celebrity crush is Taylor Swift and you hope to go to Harvard university. Of course that might have changed because you specifically said "I will go to Harvard with you since we are best friends," in the seventh grade. So yeah has anything changed?" I say. He was left shocked.

"Uh, some I guess. My celebrity crush is now Selena Gomez, I don't know which university I want to go to and my favorite colour is now blue," he says.

"Ok great, well nothing of mine has changed so we're all good," I say.

"No we aren't," Zack says. "We still need to see what each one of us do on a daily basis and why we aren't on good terms."

"Well we know one of those things," I mumble.

"Uh I guess," he says.

"Ok well today is Tuesday. I usually finish my homework at Starbucks at lunch and then I do nothing when I get home. You know except going on a run and going to to Und-" I start but stop immediately.

Oh god I almost let out my secret! I have to cover it up! Fast!

"Uh...Undertown! That's what I call the park down the road," I say. He gives me a questioning look at shrugs.

"Ok when do you go out?" he asks. I check the time.

"Now!" I say and run upstairs to change.

I change into a pink, Nike, sports bra and some black shorts that go just past booty shorts. I run back downstairs after re putting my hair into a high ponytail. Zack was there with his shirt off and waiting with his hair in a mess.

"You're coming too?" I ask.

"Uh yeah..." he says.

"Oh great!" I mumble. "Prince! Mickey! I'm going for my run!" I scream.

"Ok!" they yell back.

Zack and I walk out and run 2 miles. We ran back to the park and got some ice cream then sat at the bench.

"Ah one thing has changed," Zack says. I raise my eyebrow at him.

"You switched from vanilla to chocolate," he says.

I look at my ice cream and laugh.

"Yup! But you're still a chocolate sort of guy," I say.

"Yeah. I remember when you used to hate chocolate and I always tried to make you eat it! Remember when we went to Ben and Jerry's when we were kids?" Zack laughs.

I smile at the memory. We were best friends then. I don't respond I just stare at the ground and lick my ice creamcream.

"You gonna say something?" he asks.

"Hmm? Oh um yeah lets just go back home," I say.

"But you aren't done your ice cream," he says.

"Uh, I'm not hungry anymore," I say and throw away the chocolate goodness in the garbage.

"Um, ok?" he says and we run back.

When we got back I smelt my moms best lasagna.

"Mom?!" I scream.

"Yes hun?" she says from the kitchen.

I run to the kitchen and jump into her arms. I haven't seen her in weeks!

"Oh wow! Maybe I should make surprise visits more often!" she says with a laugh and hugs me back.

"You made your famous lasagna!" I say and she nods.

"Yeah I decided to see if I still had in me," she says. "Oh! Zack! You're here! How wonderful! Haven't seen you in ages!" my mother exclaims.

"Hey Linda, long time no see," Zack says.

Linda is my moms name if you were wondering. We sat all sat at the table and ate my mothers awesome lasagna; me, Zack, Mike, Josh, and my mom.

"So how's school?" Mom asks.

"Its great so-" I start but she cuts me off.

"I was actually asking Mike honey," mom says.

"Oh, yeah, of course," I say and pick at my food.

"Oh my god Alisha! Stop picking your food! Have I taught you anything?!" my mom cries.

I stop picking and just stare. Of course she wants to hear about the golden child. And not her other child. Jeez, they still aren't over the Stacey incident!

"So um, why did you visit?" I ask.

"Well Mike has a big game and I wanted to see it," mom says.

"Really? Well I texted and called and emailed you a thousand times about my big performances for when I sing and play the guitar. But you never seem to come. Why?" I ask.

"We never have time," she says.

"Oh really? Or is it that you still hate me for what you think I did to Stacey? Even though it was Bob's fault!" I exclaim.

"Alisha! You are not allowed to mention either of their names in this house! Especially with guests!" my mom exclaims.

"Oh no! They know everything! But I get it really! You hate your own child! Well I'm sorry I was 5 and couldn't do anything! So there! Now go! Go and be proud of the golden child. Leave me here! Because I totally don't need my mom!" I scream and run upstairs.

I slam the door shut and take out the blade again. I lock the bathroom door and cut a small cut on my wrist.

"Alisha no!" Josh screams. He busted the door open and takes the blade away from me.

"Please don't!" he pleads and washes my hand.

"She hates me!" I scream.

I get out of his grasp and open my window.

"No! Don't jump!" Josh yells. I do so anyways.

I jump on the tree and then jump down. I run to the Underworld without stopping. I wouldn't stop. I heard footsteps behind me but I thought I was just hearing things.

I entered the Underworld and everyone stared.

"Jack! Sign me up!" I scream and take of my shirt and reveal my pink, Nike, sports bra.

"Are you sure? You have quite a crowd," Jack says. I don't look around I just get into the ring.

"Jack! Now!" I say. He surrenders and gets my opponent.

I beat him up in 30 seconds because I knew his weakness from the beginning.

Everyone cheers and I head to the bar.

"Bill! Beer and coke!" I say.

He gets my drink and I sigh. I sip my drink quietly while listening to the cheering on the background.

"Well, this is interesting," I hear a familiar voice coming from behind me.

"Yes, yes it is. Looks like my 16 year old sister is drinking, and fighting!" another voice says.

"But that can't be because she would have told us," the last voice says.

I turn around and see....Mike, Josh and Zack looking at me.

"I....I....can explain!" I say.

"Ok, explain," Mike says.

They seat themselves around me so I couldn't get out.

"Dy, you alright? These boys giving you trouble?" Bill asks.

"All good Bill their...friends?" I say but sounded more like a question.

"Alright," Bill says but sounds unconvinced.

"Explain," Josh says.

"Fine! Josh remember when I told you about Danger, Ray, Edward and Chris? And Mike, remember I use to say I'm going to the mall to meet with some friends? And Zack when we were...friends....and you wanted to come over, sometimes I would say I was hanging with Ally?" I ask. They all nod.

"Well those were all...lies? Or twists of truth. I didn't tell you everything Josh. And Mike, I did meet friends just not at the mall. And Zack, what I said to you was a complete lie. I never hung out with Ally when I said that." I say.

They were all shocked. Mike and Zack more than Josh.

"So what is the truth?" Josh asks.

"Well...this is gonna be a long story!" I say.

Authors Note

Did you like it? I hope so! Are you ready to find out more about Alisha's childhood? Like who are Bill and Jack? How the guys react to everything? Well you will have to what a while. I'm sorry I'm leaving you on a cliff hanger for a long time. Probably a week or so. I'm caught up in school and all. Anyways, in the mean time read my other book, Good Girl Gone Bad!

Chapter 19

Alisha's P.O.V

"So, it all started when I was 5," I start.

"You all know what happened. Well, when I turned 10, I was sick and tired of my parents treating me so badly. So I ran away. That was the day when you, Mike, almost had a heart attack because you couldn't find me," I laugh at the memory

"Anyways, I had ran to an alley and cried my eyes out, until The Rippers found me. Josh, what I told you was true; they did help me. But not in the comforting sort of way. Instead, they brought me here, to the Underworld. They taught me what they knew about fighting, which was limited, but I still learned. Bill here, was like a dad to me. He is a professor and always helped me with homework and all. Jack over there," I say pointing to Jack who was busy announcing the next fight.

"He was also like a dad to me. He taught me everything I know about fighting. I just added a bit of..."me" in it. I'm the best fighter out of all the Rippers. I haven't lost a single fight here!" I say proudly.

"Hey, Bill, remember the fight I had with the Skeleton? He was humongous but both you and Jack said I could take him? And then I imagined him as someone I didn't like," I say looking at Zack then continue. "And I beat him up so bad that Jack had to pry me off of him? He had a concussion and we never saw him after that," I say laughing.

"Yeah I remember! I don't blame him for not coming back though, he was beaten up by a 15 year old!" He says also laughing.

"Dynamite and Hulk to the ring!" Jack announces. Hulk? Who the heck has a fight name as Hulk?

"I wonder who's up!" Mike says. I smirk.

"See you guys after I win!" I say and walk to the ring.

"Ali-" Josh stars but I cut him off.

"Down here I'm Dynamite!" I yell from behind me.

I get into the ring and examine my opponent. Right handed, strong arms, weak legs.

Block his punches Alisha. Kick him in the legs. I think to myself.

In less than a minute I put him down. Ha ha sucks for him.

"Good Job, Dy," Jack says. I smile at him and walk back to the guys.

"Well Dynamite," Josh says.

"You're quite strong. Explains how you beat me and Zack up," Josh says. I laugh and nod.

We walk out of the Underworld and back home.

"You guys can't say anything," I say turning to face them.

"Everyone in the city knows about me and how I'm the best fighter around. They just don't know who I am, what I look like. Please don't say a word. If you do, then I will be treated differently at school. People will be afraid of me and see me as a threat and I don't want that," I plead.

"We won't say a word," Zack says. I raise my eyebrow at him and he sighs.

"Just cause we aren't friends, doesn't mean I can't be nice and keep your secret," he says. I am still questioning him but I let it slide.

We walk into my driveway and enter the house. Mike and Josh go in while Zack stays out. I stand my the door just looking at him.

"Ok, look, I know the project is to see what we do on a daily basis but you can't put that in it" I say.

"I already promised you I wouldn't tell anyone. Why do you keep telling me not to say anything?" he says.

"First of all, this is the second time. Second of all, I'm just making sure. And lastly-" but I stop there.

"Lastly what?" he questions.

"You broke another big promise so why should I trust you now?" I mumble to myself. Hopefully he didn't hear that.

"You're still dwelling over that?" he asks. Guess he heard me.

"Sorry! But I have the right to not trust you! Whatever. Tomorrow is your day, I will meet you at your place after school," I say. He rolls his eyes and nods.

"Ok see you tomorrow then," he says and walks away. Jerk. Why was I ever friends with him? I don't know.

I close the door and walk into my room. I slump on my bed and curl up in a ball.

"We're going to sleep?" Josh asks.

"Yes Prince. Good night," I say and drift of into a deep slumber. The last thing I hear is Josh mumbling to himself:

"This girl is the strongest person I know,"

After that I don't know. But I'm pretty sure he also fell asleep. Good thing cause I'm tired.

Authors Note

OMG guys I'm so sorry I haven't updated in a while. Please don't hate me! It's just school has been drowning me in work. Anyways I know its a short chapter but I really wanted something up for you guys. Hope you enjoyed and don't forget to read my other book Good Girl Gone Bad.

Thanks and Love you!!

Chapter 20

Alisha's P.O.V

Guess what today is? Another day spent with my ex-bestfriend! Yay! Not. I had went to school and now I'm driving back to my house with the radio blasting music.

"Mmmm whatcha say? Mmmm that you only meant wellWell of course you didMmmm whatcha say? Mmmm that you its all for the best!"

Yes. I'm listening to Jason Derulo. I love this song.

I'm driving back to my house at the moment. I don't understand why we have to do this stupid project. And with him?! I swear that teacher is out to get me.

I pull up into my driveway and get out of the car. I go to the backyard and look at the gate I thought I'd never use again. I sigh and open it up.

I walk into his backyard and take everything in. It looks the same as always. Tulips on the left, roses on the right. I walk to the door and knock three times. Zack comes into view and he open up the door.

"Come on in," he says and moves to the side to give me some room. I walk in and head towards the living room. His house hasn't changed at all. I set my bag down and sit on the couch making myslef comfortable.

"Shall we get started?" I ask.

"Sure. So today is what? Wednesday? I usually having boxing today, Thursdays and Mondays. The rest of the week I'm free and I don't do anything." Zack says.

I nod.

"So when do you leave for boxing?" I ask.

He checks the clock and looks back at me.

"In 30 minutes," he says.

"Great. Let's watch TV while we wait," I say. He shrugs and we go along and watch TV.

30 minutes later, Zack is holding his car keys and a bag in his hands while we head to his car. We get in and he drives for 10 minutes to his practice.

"I don't want to ask you for any favors but could you teach me some fighting tricks?" He asks.

"I thought boxing was only punching," I say.

"It is but from what I saw yesterday, you have a pretty strong punch. Please?" He pleads.

"Um...ok," I say unsure.

Zack stops the car in front of an old building.

"Here it is! Let's go," he says.

We go inside and into a ring. There were 3 rings and apparently, Zack reserved a ring for us before we left.

At first I let him at me but I blocked all his punches. I taught him how to punch powerfully, how to avoid punches and how to act fast. Obviously I taught him the lowest tricks I knew because I didn't want him abusing me with my own tricks.

1 hour later we were both panting.

"Wow, you're a hard core coach," Zack says.

I shrug. My phone starts to ring and I look at the caller ID. It was Josh.

"Hello?" I say.

"Alisha? Oh my god where are you?" Josh questions.

"With Zack," I say.

"ALONE?!" Josh screams.

"Yes. We are working on the project," I say calmly.

"Is he being abusive?" Josh asks.

I roll my eyes.

"No,"

"Are you sure? "

"Yes, now I gotta go. See you in like 30 minutes." I say and with that I end the call.

"What was that all about?" Zack asks while sipping his water.

"Just Josh acting like an protective boyfriend ," I say with a shrug.

"You know he likes you right?" Zack says.

"As if!" I say.

"It's true!" Zack defends.

"Mmhmm sure. I'm hungry let's go eat," I say hoping to change the subject.

He let's the subject slide and we head off to eat. We ended up stopping by Harveys and picked up 2 burgers. They were delicious!

Now we're headed back to our houses. We pulled up into Zack's drive way and got out of the car. We walked to the backyard and he opened the gate for me.

"See you tomorrow I guess?" I ask.

"My schedule is the same tomorrow so unless you want to do the exact same thing, there's no point." Zack says. I nod.

"OK, Friday then?" I ask. He nods.

"Bye Zack," I say quietly and head into my backyard.

I don't think I heard him correctly, but I think I heard him say...

"Good night Lila."

He closes the door and I go into my house and climb the stairs to my room.

Josh was laying on my bed, looking at his phone.

"I'm home!" I say.

"Oh thank god! I thought he rapped you!" Josh exclaims. I roll my eyes and drop on the bed. He's just being dramatic.

"Alisha is tired. She wants to go to bed," I mumble into my pillow.

"OK princess. Night," Josh says.

The lights turn off and the bed dips like usual. I fall into a deep slumber instantly.

Authors Note

Short chapter I know. The book is gonna be finishing soon. Hopefully at chapter 35. I don't know though. I hope you guys are liking it so far though. Anyways, do you ship Jolisha or Aliak? Tell me what you think in the comments! And don't forget to vote! Thanks! Love you!!

Chapter 21

Josh's P.O.V

I'm convinced Zack is going to kill Alisha. Why? I don't know. I want to keep them away from each other but I can't or else she will fail her project. That can't happen or else we will kill me. And since she's a fighter, I think she can actually kill me.

Her eyes were closed and her soft hair covered her face. I could hear her quiet breathing. She started to shake and I knew right then she was having a bad dream. Probably another one about Zack.

I hated that man. I called him my best friend once. I can't believe I thought he was a good guy. Abusing a girl is not a good thing. Not to mention he coukd have gone to jail if Alisha called the cops! But she didn't vecause she cared for him. And he betrayed her And for such a long time? I still can't believe she's been hurt so many times by so many people she trusted. I mean she must have really bad trust issues.

Not to mention her parents! Blaming her for something she didn't do! They should be mad at her uncle! She's had a terrible life. The death of a sister. 3 friends leaving her. Her parents mad at her for no damn reason. That's pretty harsh.

I held her close to me and tried to keep her calm. She dug her face into my shirt and after a few minutes she stopped shaking. We stayed like that for a while. It felt right. Cliché, I know...

I drifted of to sleep when I finally put my mind at ease that she'd be okay. And if she isn't, well she can handle herself. And if she can't she has me, Mike and the rest of the guys.

I kissed her cheek ad smiled. Then I wen to bed.

The next morning Alisha did her usual routine. Got up, took a shower, changed (in the bathroom unfortunately), did her makeup then went down to her car and drove to Starbucks.

She is in love with that place, I swear.

I get to school and look for Zack. I see him sucking some cheerleader'd face. I pull him off and slam him into the lockers. He grunys but I didn't care.

"Listen here you. If you hurt Alisha you're a dead man. It's not a threat its a promise. If she comes home crying because of you, you're so screwed. Got it?" I say through gritted teeth. I was raging right now.

"Wow, you're whipped man," Zack says with a smirk. I slam him harder against the lockers and he grunts again. He's lucky I'm not giving him a concussion!

"Shut up. If you know whats good for you, you will be good to her. I don't know why she put up with you for all those years. She should have called the cops on you a long time ago but she didn't. You should be so grateful. She did nothing to you! She's a kind, sweet, intelligent and strong girl.

You're a coward. You should be ashamed that you let a girl like Aliha go," I say.

By this point, we gathered a crowd. I let go of him and glared. I stomped away to my class. And as I was walking, that's when I realized I liked Alisha.

I liked Alisha Johnson.

The nerdy, good two shoes, who put up a disguise to cover up her real self. I like the girl who gave me a roof over my head and let me live in her house.

I liked everything about her. Her smile, blush, laugh, giggle. She was different. And I know, so cliché right? But she was different because she had a little bit of everything. She was fit like the cheerleaders. Smart like a nerd. Strong like a gangster. She was like the perfect girl. Other than her insecurities. Buy those also made her original, unique and cute.

Oh my god.I don't like Alisha.

I'm in love with her.

And the worst part is, I was falling harder for her every single day.

Zack's P.O.V

His words echoed in my ears.

"She did nothing to you!"

"You should be ashamed that you let a girl like Alisha go,"

All the words were in my head. I slammed a locker and held my head in my hands.

I should be ashamed. I let our friendship go for a stupid reason. And I needed to tell her why.

We were done the most part of our project. It's just the why we aren't on good terms. She thinks she knows but she doesn't.

I walked to her class and waited till the bell rang to tell her to come over today. I know I told her to come tomorrow but I needed to tell her today. I will just move around my schedule.

The bell rang and people started filling the halls. Alisha took a little longer to get her things. When she walked out I pulled her arm and turned her to face me.

"What the hell Zack?" She says.

"Sorry. I just wanted to say you have to come over today," I say.

"But I thought you said-," she started but I cut her off.

"Yeah I know what I said but who cares. Come over after school okay?" I say urging her to agree.

She sighs, rolls her eys and nods her head. I let her go and she rushes of to her next class. I smile. I remember how she hates being late. I miss Alisha in my life.

I should have never let her go. I am an idiot.

Authors Note

Hey guys! Did you like the chapter? Now are you ready to find out why Zack let Alisha go? Well stay tuned for the next chapter which will probably be up soon. Please read my other story too Good Girl Gone Bad! Thanks! And don't forget to comment and vote!

Chapter 22

Alisha's P.O.V

Zack asked me to come over. And yesterday he said not to. What the actual hell? I was gonna go to the Underworld but now I can't! What's up with this guy?

I turned on my phone and called Josh.

"Hello?" His voice says.

"Hi," I say.

"Hey Princess what's up?" Josh asks.

"I've gotta cancel our plans. Zack has something important to tell me so I have to go over to his place," I say.

"What? No!" Josh whines. Awe he sounded like a child.

"Don't worry, when I get back we can watch a movie and cuddle or whatever," I say.

"Hmmm, I guess that could make up for it," Josh says. I giggle.

"Ok Prince, I'll see you tonight," I say.

"Bye Princess," Josh says and with that I hang up the phone.

I walked to my car because it was the end of the day, and drove to Zack's house. I parked in his drive way and sat there in my seat.

What does he want to tell me? I ask myself.

Well go inside and find out stupid! My brain says.

I sigh and get out of the car. I knock on his door and in a second the door is opened and I'm pulled inside.

"You're here!" Zack exclaims.

"Yeah!" I exclaim.

"Uh...sit down," he says.

I walk to the living room and sit down on the couch.

Zack sat down on the other couch and looked uncomfortable.

"Is everything alright?" I ask.

"To be honest, no," Zack says with a sigh.

We sat in an awkward silence for a few minutes.

Well is he gonna say anything?

"Alright, here I go," he starts.

"You probably remember the end of freshman year when, we, uh, stopped being friends," Zack says.

I nod. No duh! He almost killed me!

"Yeah well uh, I was mad at you for all the wrong reasons," he says.

I raise my eyebrow at him. I thought he didn't like me because I was ugly, annoying and fat.

"Alisha, let me ask you something. When was the last time you saw my parents?" Zack asks.

"What does that have to do with anything?" I ask.

"Just answer the question!" Zack snaps. I sigh and respond.

"I don't know. 2 years ago," I say.

"Alisha, there's a reason for that," Zack says.

I'm so confused right now.

"Zack just please tell me," I say.

"Ok. At the end of freshman year, Nina held a big party right? And she invited you, me, Ally and a bunch of other people. You called and asked if my parents could give you a ride and they said yes," Zack starts.

I nod. Yeah I remember that. I motion him to go on.

"Alisha, while we were driving to your house something happened. And it wasn't exactly good," Zack says.

His eyes were filled with hurt and sadness. Wait...no. No way was he going to say that. No!

"A drunk driver swerved into our lane and crashed into it," Zack chocked out. He had tears spilling out. His parents were dead? No!

"Zack, I'm so-" I started but he cut me off.

"No! I don't want your pity!" Zack yelled. I was taken back but understood.

"I blamed it on you! Because you we the one who called! I survived because I was at the back! My parents didn't! I should have been the one to die! Not them!" Zack cried.

He jumped out of his chair and yelled.

"They told me they'd be there forever. And then you called and now their gone!" He kept yelling.

Tears welled up in my eyes. No wonder he hates me. He blames me for his parents death.

"Zack I, " I started.

"No Alisha! I'm a terrible perosn! I blamed my best friend for something she didn't do! And I lost her because of my stupidity! I'm a horrible human being! My parents must be ashamed!" He cries and then sits on the floor.

I sat down beside him and hugged him.

"It's ok, I understand," I say.

"No its not! I shouldn't have blamed you. I blame myself. I should have said no to you. Maybe they'd still be here," Zack sighs. He was calming down.

"Zack, you were 14. You didn't know how to deal with it! Honestly, I'm glad you took it out on me. If you couldn't take it out on yourself, I'm glad you took it out on me. Your best friend," I say with a sad smile.

We sat on the floor just hugging each other for a while until I got up and held my hand down for him. Zack looked confused but took it. I helped him up and he still gave me a questioning look.

"I'm taking you somewhere," I say.

"Lila I don't," But I cut him off.

"No buts, no don'ts, just come on," I say.

I grab his hand and drag him to my car. He gets into the passenger seat and I get into the drivers seat. I start the engine and ride along the road.

"You know Josh likes you right?" Zack blurts out.

"Huh?" I ask in disbelieve.

"Yeah. He can't stop talking about you. It's his only subject i swear," Zack says with a small laugh.

"Really?" I say.

"Yes," Zack says.

I smile and blush. Wow...he likes me? My crush likes me?

"He dies over that blush," Zack says with a grin.

Even more heat rises to my cheeks. Well this is awkward.

We ride off for an hour in silence until I break it.

"Who has been taking care of you?" I ask. It almost came out as a whisper.

"Uncle Rodney and my aunt," Zack says.

I nod and sigh. Finally we see the cemetery. I look to Zack and his face drops. I knew this was the cemetery the were because it was closer to our houses.

"Alisha wha..what?" He stutters.

"I wanted to say goodbye because I didn't exactly get to. And I think you need to see them too," I say with tears rolling down my cheeks.

I refused to sob or cry. I needed to be strong for him. I just let the tears silently fall. We both got out of the car and walked to their graves. I kneel down and the tears fall.

"Hey Mr and Mrs. Alexander. It's uh me, Alisha. You know, Zack's best friend. I'm sorry I didn't come to your funeral, I didn't exactly know. But please don't be mad at Zack. He was hurting and grieving. I forgive him and I know you do too. I just thought he could talk to you guys, to let go," my voice breaks.

I sob a little and stand up wiping the tears. They were like my second parents. I loved them just as much. Since my parents weren't home, they took care of me and Mike.

Zack hugged me and then we broke apart.

"Hey mom, dad. I'm sorry I haven't been here for so long. 2 years to be exact. I've been such a terrible son huh? I'm sorry about that too. It should have been me. Not you guys," he starts.

"Why did you leave me? Was I to much to handle? Why couldn't you hold on for a little bit longer! The doctors could have saved you! But you let go! Just like that! Did you think of me at all? Cause I sure as hell thought of you! Why? WHY?" Zack yelled.

He broke out in tears. For the first time in a long time, I saw a heartbroken boy. My heartbroken best friend. I pulled him into a hug and let him cry on my shoulder while I let tears fall.

After 10 minutes, we went back to the car and hit the road.

"Thank you Alisha," Zack says.

I smile and keep my eyes on the road.

"Anytime Zack," I say and sigh.

Authors Note

Hey guys! So did you like the chapter? Plot twist huh? Did you see that coming? This is why Zack hated Alisha. Told you there was more then 1 reason! Anyways, the book is coming to an end and I'm sort of sad. Hope you guys enjoy the last few chapters!

Chapter 23

Josh's P.O.V

Alisha cancelled on our date. I was so looking forward to it. But of course Zack had to take her away. Honestly, I hate that kid at the moment. I mean what's his deal? One minute he hates her, the next minute he's all over her.

I even told him I liked her. Why did I do that? Because I thought we were friends. I mean I'm not in love with her. But I like her...a lot.

I go crazy for her smile and her perfectly aligned, white, teeth. Not to mention her crazy blush she does when she's embarrassed. God, it's the perfect shade of pink on her. Her eyes sparkle when she's happy, which is almost never, and her hair is so gorgeous.

But what I honestly love about her, is that she is perfect. And not perfect as in she has perfect teeth, hair, eyes etc. Even though she does. No. Perfect as in she knows her imperfections and her flaws. Yet she chooses to own it all and not give a damn about what people think about her. I mean she is insecure, but I know deep down she loves herself.

I just want to protect her, if I'm being completely honest here. After I saw her cut herself, twice, and after I saw what she did in her spare time, I saw a whole new side of her. One that was hurting yet strong. I could see the glint of adventure when she was in the ring and that she just wanted to be free.

Then we come back to her past and her parents. I still can't wrap my head around all that. Her sister's death, her uncle, her parents blaming her. It's just all so much. And the fact that Nina left her. That sucks too. If one of my friends left me, I would be real pissed.

"Josh?" I hear Alisha's voice.

I rush out of the living room and see her beautiful face standing at the door.

"Hey, how was your meeting with Zack?" I ask.

"It was great. We actually made up," she says.

What? They made up. By force? Or my want?

"Wait what?" I ask.

"I know, I'm in shock too, but we did," she says.

"H-how?" I ask.

"I don't know if I should tell. Um do you know what happened to Zack's parents?" She says sadly.

"Of course. They died 2 years ago," I say.

Alisha's face drops slightly and her eyes began to water. Oh no. She was going to cry.

"Yeah, well at the end of freshman year, Zack and his parents were gonna pick my up and drop me and Zack at Nina's place for an end of the year party. And on the way to my place they got into a car crash. And Zack blamed me," Alisha says. She choked on a few words and tears began to fall. But she pretended she didn't notice.

"He felt so bad when I went over. He screamed how he was a terrible person for blaming me. But I forgave him. He was only 14 and was confused. I can't hold it against him. We went to the cemetery to pay our respects and then I came here," she says.

She began to cry and I went up to her and hugged her. Her small body cried into my shirt and was shaking. I set her on the couch and just held her.

"It's ok. Everything is gonna be okay," I say to try and calm her down.

"They were like second parents to me. Real parents who loved me," she says.

I nod and stroke her hair. She had finally stopped crying and we just laid there and cuddled.

3 hours later she wad fast asleep..I carried her upstairs and set her down on the bed.

The next morning, we got up and just laid there.

"I don't want to go to school," Alisha says. I laugh.

"Miss. Goodie goodie doesn't want to go to school?" I say with humor in my voice.

She sits up and slaps me across the chest, then smiles.

"I think you and I both know I'm anything but a goodie goodie. Doing illegal fighting isn't exactly good," she says. I raise my hands in surrender.

"Yes you're right. My apologies princess," I say.

She laughs and lies back down.

"So what do you wanna do today?" I ask. I sit up and lean on my side keeping my weight on my arm.

"Mmmm sleep," Alisha responds.

"Or..." I say. Then I tickle her.

She screams and laughs. I smile while tickling her.

"Josh! Hahaha! Stop! Hahaha!" She pleads.

I laugh and stop tickling her so she can catch her breath.

"So...what do you want to do?" I ask innocently.

"Um...I don't know," she responds.

"Well there is the amusement park, and since everyone is at school or at work, we could go on all the rides!" I suggest.

Her eyes lite up like a Christmas tree. She nods her head frantically and quickly stands up.

"Yeah! Yeah! Yeah!" She cries and jumps up and down like a child. I laugh and lie back down.

"No time for lying down lazy butt! Up! Up!" Alisha says and tries to pull my arm. Key word: tries.

"Ok! Ok!" I say and get up. I stretch my arms and walk to her drawers. There's one specific drawer with all my clothes.

Alisha goes to the bath room and I change. Ten minutes later, she is out wearing a white, slightly cropped, tank top, with an infinity sign on it and says Love. She wears some ripped jean shorts and pairs it with some black, vans.

Her hair was wavy and fell perfectly onto her shoulders and over all she looked beautiful.

"You done checking me out?" She asks with a smirk.

"Uh yeah? I mean no! I mean...let's go!" I say. I take her hand and we go. Well, after she takes her phone, purse and wallet.

We get onto my motorcycle and drive to the amusement park. An hour later, we arrived at Disneyland.

"Oh. My. God. Disneyland?! I have never been here before!" Alisha squeals. My eyes widen.

"Never," I ask.

"Never," she says.

I shake my head, grab her hand, and rush her off to security. Once we were done, and paid for our ticket, we entered the park. Well one of them.

There was no one here. I mean a few infants and their families but other than that, no one.

"We have to go on all the rides," I say.

She nods her head and we were off.

~6 hours later~

We went to every park and on every ride. There were no line ups at all. It was epic. Now we were going on the ferris wheel. I saved that for last. Now I know this sounds cliché and it probably will become a cliché moment, but I don't care.

THE GOOD GIRL

The sun was setting and we went into our cage? I guess you could call it. We were going up and Alisha was amazed by the sunset. It was pink and purple and over all wonderful.

"It's so beautiful," she says.

"Just like you," I say.

She turns around and we make eye contact. Her cheeks start to get pink and I walk over to her. I grab her waist, pull her closer towards me and and softly put a kiss on her lips. She smiles and kisses me back.

We were at the top by now and I bent down on one knee. Alisha's eyes widened.

"Alisha, you're an amazing, strong and beautiful girl. I go crazy for that blush and that smile of yours. Your imperfections make you perfect and the way you fight is quite the turn on," I start.

She giggles.

"That giggle of yours is music to my ears and the way your eyes light up when you're happy or excited is so cute. Just like you. I know at first, you didn't exactly trust me. But over time, I'm glad you did. You let me in when you were hurting and I'm forever grateful for that. Please make me the happiest man on earth and...become my girlfriend?" I ask.

I pull out a small box and open it. It reveals a promise ring.

"This promise ring is my promise to you that I will never hurt you and I will always love you," I say.

Those last 5 words both our eyes widen. I just said I love her. Oh no.

"I love you too," she whispers and looks down at her feet.

I stand up and put my finger under her chin to make her look at me. I take her ring finger, put the ring on and kiss her gently. She responds and after that, the ride come to an end. Talk about perfect timing.

We get out hand in hand and walk to my motorcycle. By now, it was 7. When we got home it was 8. And Alisha was tired.

I carried her to her bed room and set her on her bed...again.

"I promise," she says under her breath and falls back asleep.

I smile. I just got the girl of my dreams!

I lay down next to her and sigh.

Today was a good day. A very good day.

Authors Note

Hey guys! I finally got to the part where they admit there love for each other. Yay! I hope you guys liked it. Can't wait for the next chapter! Don't forget to check out my new book Good Girl Gone Bad!

Chapter 24

Alisha's P.O.V

I woke up with a smile on my face. Josh is my boyfriend! It feels amazing! I turn my body to face him and he was awake.

"Hey Princess," he says in his morning voice.

"Hi Prince," I say.

"We gotta get ready for school," Josh says with a sigh.

"Unfortunately," I add.

Josh chuckles and shakes his head. We both get out of bed and I go to my closet and take out some sweatpants and a baggy top.

"You're wearing that?" Josh exclaims.

"Yup!" I say popping the "p".

"Do you want people to think your depressed?" Josh says.

I roll my eyes.

"No one will think I'm depressed," I say.

"Uh yeah they will!" Josh exclaims.

I sigh and put my hands on my hips.

"Fine, then you pick out my outfit, boyfriend," I say with a smirk.

"Okay, girlfriend," Josh says with a smirk.

I go to the bathroom and brush my teeth and do my hair. I come out and see Josh holding my outfit.

It was some black leggings and a green crop top that will surely show just a little bit over my belly button. He paired it with some accessories and combat boots. I raise my eyebrow at him.

"So you want me to dress like Rebecca?" I ask.

"No. Rebecca wears tube tops and mini mini skirts. You're just wearing a crop top and leggings," Josh replies.

I raise my hands in surrender and take the clothes. Then I order him to go into the bathroom so I can change.

I quickly slip everything on and look at myself in the mirror. Wow. I actually look good. I mean I would wear this, just not on a regular school day. I wonder what everyone will think. But I shouldn't care what they think...right?

Josh comes out and looks at me.

"Damn! I have a hot girlfriend," he says.

I blush and smile.

"Thanks," I say.

He opens his arms and I walk over and hug him. His cologne scent was heavenly. We pull apart and I go downstairs to eat breakfast while he changes.

"So what's going on between you and Josh?" Mike's voice says.

I spin around and see him leaving against the wall.

"Um, we're dating?" I say but it came out more as a question.

"And when were you planning on telling me?" Mike asks and starts coming towards me.

"Uh, we only got together yesterday!" I say in defense.

"I see. Is that why you weren't at school yesterday?" Mike asks.

"You noticed?" I ask.

"Yes. Now answer my question," Mike says.

"Yes," I say.

"I see. Alright, I'm fine with you dating but no funny business okay?" Mike says.

I nod.

"And when you do the dirty, make sure you lock your door," Mike says with a smirk.

My jaw drops open and my eyes widen. Mike laughs and walks out the door.

"Hey, why's your face in shock mode?" Josh asks while coming into the kitchen.

"My brother just gave me permission to have sex with you," I say dumfounded.

Josh spits out his OJ and laughs.

"Joshua! That's isn't funny!" I say.

"Sorry!" He says and cleans up his mess.

We head outside and into his car.

"I'm not looking forward to school," I say.

"Why?" Josh asks.

"Because gossip spreads like a wild fire there, everyone will know we are dating by first period! And I'm not ashamed of you its just I hate being the centre of attention," I explain.

"Babe chill. If anyone is giving you troubles I will work something out with them," Josh days and pulls up into the parking lot.

"Well you better work something out now because here comes your fan club!" I say and then I get out of the car.

I was eyed by everyone. The guys and especially the girls. Some guys were giving me evil smirks, others were just shaking their heads. Girls were looking at me in disgust, and let me tell you, it was uncomfortable.

I slung my heavy backpack over my shoulders and proceeded to walk into school. Zack was standing at my locker.

"So I heard you slept with Josh," he says.

"ZACHARY!" I scream then slap his chest.

"Jesus Christ women! I didn't say I believed them!" He says. I gave him the-seriously-face.

"Okay maybe I belived it a little," he admits. I shake my head.

"Zack I promise I didn't sleep sleep with him. I mean we slept in the same bed, but nothing happened! We just started dating yesterday!" I explain.

"Whatever you say!" He sings.

I sigh and put in my locker combination.

"Hey babe," Josh says and kisses my cheek.

"Hi," I say and look at Zack.

Oh no. Please don't start a fight.

"Josh, I know you can't trust me like you use to but can we please start over?" Zack asks.

"I don't know," Josh says and looks at me.

"Come on Josh! You guys were such good friends before me!" I say.

"Okat fine, I forgive you Zack," Josh says with a small smile.

"Thanks man," Zack says and runs a finger through his hair.

I smile then the bell rings.

"Well I gotta go, see you guys later," I say and walk to my class.

Suddenly I hear familiar clicks of stilettos. Shoot! Rebecca!

"ALISHA!" She screeches.

Shoot! Shoot! Shoot! I'm dead.

She walks towards me and yanks my hair.

"Ow," I scream.

"You're a nasty little girl you know that? Sleeping with my boyfriend! Who the hell do you think you are?" She says and yanks my hair again.

"Stop!" I plead.

"No! I'm gonna do something I should have done a long time ago. You're dead," she threatens and throws me against the locker.

We've gathered a crowd and no one is doing anything about it. Her minions come and pin me to the wall. She proceeds to punch, kick and slap me. Her minions nails dig into my skin and start drawing blood.

"Stop!" I plead.

"No!" Rebecca yells.

She grabs my throat and I start to choke.

"Stop!" I plead with my voice sounding hoarse.

"What's going on here?" The principals voice booms.

Rebecca and her minions let go of me and have panic faces. I drop to the floor and cough but it hurt.

"Alisha!" I hear Josh's voice from the hallway.

"Josh," I whisper.

Keep your eyes open. Keep your eyes open. Come on! Hold on!

I told myself.

"Alisha don't close your eyes," Josh pleads.

"Im tired. But I won't," I say.

I feel myself being elevated from the floor and into some strong arms. My vision became blurry and I started to get a massive headache. Suddenly, my eyes fell shut and I drifted off to sleep.

Chapter 25

Josh's P.O.V

Alisha is in the hospital right now. They doctors said she might never wake up! And it's all my fault. How? Because Rebecca is madly in love with me and basically killed my Alisha! If Rebecca would have just never liked me then this would have never happened.

"Dude, it's not your fault," Mike says.

"Mike it is!" I say.

"No its not! It's that stupid Rebecca's fault!" Zack exclaims.

"But if she wasn't madly in love with me, Alisha wouldn't be in a coma right now!" I exclaim.

"It's ok! She's strong! I mean, she's been an illegal street fighter for 6 years!" Mike says.

I hope he's right. She has to be okay. Suddenly, a bunch of doctors run into Alisha's hospital room.

"What's going on?" I ask one of them.

"Her heart race is beating fast, it's like she's worried or getting an anxiety attack in her sleep and she won't wake up. If it keeps going on, and we can't lower it, we'll have to put her down," she says the last part in a whisper.

"No! Can't you do something?" I ask.

"The only thing we can do is have someone come in and comfort her. Maybe then she will calm down," she suggests.

I thought about it. I might as well.

"I'll do it," I say.

"Really?" She asks.

"I'm her boyfriend!" I retort.

"Alright," she says and let's me in.

I walk in and see Alisha sweating and her heart rate up. I walk over to her and the doctors leave. I hold her hand and sigh.

"Alisha don't worry. Please calm down. I know when you get like this it's about school, your family or your past but please stop worrying. Nothing is going to happen so long as I'm here. I won't leave you and I will never let Rebecca hurt you again. Please wake up. Don't let them give up on you. Mike needs you. Ally needs you. I need you. You can't leave. Not today. Please come back! Don't leave me. Don't give up," I say.

I just stare at her for a few minutes and suddenly the heart monitor goes to a normal pace. I smile and then I feel slight movement from Alisha.

"Lila?" I whisper.

"Josh?" She whispers back.

"Oh my god. You're alive!" I exclaim.

"Yeah, I guess I am," she says with a small chuckle.

"I'll get the doctors," I say.

"Wait!" Alisha says and grabs my hand.

"Yeah," I say.

"Thank you," she says with a smile.

"For what?" I ask and sit back down on the chair.

"For calming me down. If it wasn't for you I would have just gave up," she responds.

I smile and kiss her.

"Princess, anything for you," I say.

She smiles back and blushes. I love that blush! I walk out and get the doctors.

"She's awake?" Mike exclaims.

"Yup," I say.

"I guess you did it," Zack says.

"Yeah, I guess I did," I say with a smile.

"So do you know when we can see her?" Mike asks. He tries to hide it but I know he's anxious to see his little sister.

"I guess we can go in now," I respond.

We go into the room and the doctors are hovered over her. One of them walks over to us.

"She lost a lot of blood but she is still sturdy. She has a minor concussion so no school for her for 2 weeks. And with homework and whatnot, she will not be allowed to do that," he doctor says.

"How is she suppose to be caught up then?" Zack asks.

"Guys don't worry. The good thing about being a nerd is that you're always 4 steps ahead of the class. I know the rest of the material for each class to last the whole year. 2 weeks is nothing," Alisha says.

"Alisha!" Mike exclaims and runs over to hug her.

"Mike! I'm fine," she says and hugs him back.

"You're fine? You were almost killed," he says.

"Well I'm not dead and that's all that matters," Alisha says. "What happened after I passed out?"

"Rebecca and the rest of her posy went to the principals office and they are expelled and are going to jail for criminal offense. But, knowing Rebecca and her wealth, her dad probably bailed her out into doing community service or whatnot. We rushed you to the hospital and my phone has been blowing up with texts and calls from Nina. She was absent today and didn't know Rebecca was gonna do all that to you," I say.

"Wow," is all Alisha says.

"Alisha, next time some dimwitt decides to hurt you, just hurt them back," Zack says. She nods.

"Well there isn't gonna be a next time because we are gonna stand by you at all times," Mike says.

"Mike, that's not necessary," Alisha sighs.

"Yes it is little sis because honestly, I don't want to lose another sister," Mike whispers the last part.

"You're not gonna lose me," Alisha says sternly.

"I know," Mike says with a smile and kisses her forehead.

"So, what did you dream about?" Zack asks.

"Oh....nothing," Alisha says and looks down.

"Really? Because you had an anxiety attack in your sleep," Zack emphasizes sleep.

"Alright, I'll tell you. You might think I've gone insane but trust me, it's all legit," she says.

We nod and get comfy.

"Alright, here it goes," and she starts.

And that's when she told us her story.

Chapter 26

Alisha's P.O.V

"When I fell asleep there were two people who were in front of me. One being Uncle Bob and the other...Stacey," I start with a sigh.

"Both of them were there and, Uncle Bob replayed all my worst moments in life. When Stacey died, when my parents left for the first time. When Nina and Ally left. When Zack left. When the Rippers left. Everything. All the memories I wanted to lock away forever were suddenly replayed in front of me! Do you know how traumatizing that is? I could barely deal with them individually. Dealing with them all at once was terrifying," I say.

"Is that why you started to have a panic attack?" Josh asks.

"Yeah. Then Stacey showed me all my good moments in life. When Mike came to my first concert, when Nina and I made up, when I met you Josh, when we admitted we liked each other, and when me and Zack made up! At that point I was still having a panic attack. Stacey opened up one portal and Bob opened up another. Stacey's portal led to the real world and Bob's portal led to the afterlife. At first I was gonna go with Bob. The look on Stacey's face was terrifying. But then I heard a voice. At first I thought it was Stacey, but it turned out to be you Josh. You convinced me to stay. So I went with Stacey. She wanted me to tell you, Mike, that she loves and misses you. And she wanted me to tell you two," I say pointing at Josh and Zack, "to be good to me or else she will haunt you," I finish.

They all looked shocked.

"That really happened?" Mike asks. I nod.

"You actually saw Stacey?" Mike asks. I nod.

"Stacey actually said that?" Mike asks again. I nod.

"Wow," is all Mike says after that.

"Did you see anyone else?" Zack asks.

"Yes Zack, I saw your parents," I start.

"Are they mad at me?" He asks and puts his head into his hand.

"No. They wanted me to tell you that they are proud you fixed things and admitted your mistakes. They wished they could be here," I finish.

Zack started to get teary eyed. Tears started to spill but he ignored it. He just smiled.

"Well I'm glad you're okay," Josh says.

"Me two," Mike says.

"Me three," Zack says. We laugh and the room falls into a comfortable silence.

Soon after, a doctor comes in to check on me.

"We will keep you here for the night and hopefully you can go home tomorrow afternoon," the doctor says.

"Alright, thank you," I respond with a smile. She walks to the door and looks up from her clipboard.

"Visiting hours are almost up. You three will have to leave soon," the doctor says. The guys mumble a few "fine", "whatever" and "really?" But they nod.

"I will see you guys tomorrow okay?" I say. They nod and leave.

The next morning I woke up to see a nurse looking at me.

"Good morning honey. How are you feeling?" She asks.

"Other then a headache and starvation, fine," I say.

"Well I can cure one of those things right now," she says with a small chuckle and hands me some soup.

"When you're done, the doctor will come in to check up on you and you will be able to leave if he says so. Alright?" The nurse says. I nod.

She leaves the room and I'm left bored. I eat my soup in silence and just think.

My life has changed a lot. I got a boyfriend, Zack and I made up, Nina and I made up. But some things still remain the same.

Come to think of it, I didn't even know Uncle Bob was dead. I thought he was in jail...I guess he died. But my parents would have known about it...then why didn't they tell me?

"Because they love you," a voice says. I turn my head around to see Stacey.

"S-S-Stacey?" I whisper.

"Hey little sis," she says and sits on the bed.

"But how?" I ask.

"I only have a little time left here. They let me come and talk to you," she responds.

"They?" I ask.

"The leaders of the afterlife. Anyways, how are you holding up?" She asks.

"Okay I guess," I say.

"Thats good," she says.

A few moments later I sigh.

"Why did you leave me?" I ask.

"Alisha, I never wanted too. But it happened. It was my time. But I always looked after you. Whenever you felt down and you called my name, I sat there listening to you rant. I wanted to help you but I couldn't. I'm so sorry," Stacey says with a small sob.

"Why does mom and dad hate me?" I ask.

"They don't hate you. They are still confused about everything. Give them a bit more time," Stacey says. I nod.

"But I've given them almost 12 years," I say.

"I know. They'll come around. I promise," Stacey says. I nod again.

"Hey, you're graduating in a year huh?" Stacey asks. I shrug.

"I suppose," I say.

"Well congrats," she says.

"Well I'm not graduating this year, Mike is," I say.

"Oh right," Stacey says.

"Say congratulations to him for me," she says and starts to fade.

"I will. But uh what's happening to you?" I ask while holding back a sob.

"They are pulling me back," she says and gets up.

"No Stacey don't go!" I cry.

"I'm sorry! I love you Alisha. I will always be there for you," she says and hugs me.

"I love you too," I say and hug her back.

"Goodbye," she says. And faded away.

"Goodbye," I say with are a sigh.

I sat there. Quietly. Processing what happened. I got to say goodbye to my sister. For real. I finally got closure. Something I've wanted for a long time. And damn, it felt good.

Chapter 27

Alisha's P.O.V

The next day I was let out. Thank god! Hospitals make me feel depressed. Believe me when I say if I had a hospital, I would make it way more fun. The walls would be blue, and each room would be for a specific person. For example a kids room would be blue, with a painting of a sun, flowers etc. Then there would be toys so they aren't bored to death. And there would be a tv. Or for a teenager, a more subtle colour like white. And there would be a TV and an Xbox. Yeah I think big!

The guys came to pick me up. Apparently, they were here since 8 am while I was sleeping! I woke up 3 hours later. Don't judge! I was tired.

I walked into my room and smiled. My room looks way better than a hospital room. I decided I would go to the Underworld. Not for fighting, just to practice and to see people.

I get changed and I head downstairs. Luckily the guys are at football practice at the moment and Josh is at Luca's house with the guys. They said they wanted me to rest. They won't be home for a good 2 hours and I will only be staying there for 1.

I go out and start to run to the Underworld. I'm out of shape so running would help me get back on track. I got there and entered. Bill was the first one to see me and his eyes lit up with joy.

"Dynamite!" He screams. I smile and head towards the bar where a Coke Cola was waiting for me.

"Hey Bill," I say and hug him.

He hugs me back and kisses my forehead.

"Where have you been?" He asks.

"Oh you know, I just got beat up multiple times so I had to go to the hospital. But I'm all good," I say simply.

"Who put you in the hospital?" Jack exclaims from behind me. I turn around and sure enough he's there.

"Hey Jack!" I say trying to change the subject.

"Don't 'hey Jack' me. Who put you in the hospital?" He asks again. I sigh.

"Rebecca," I mumble.

"That girl is gonna get it from me!" Jack exclaims.

"No its ok! She's in jail!" I say. He sighs and relaxes his muscles.

"Good. Anyways, hey Dy," he says and hugs me. I hug him back and he also issues my forehead.

"Just so you know, you won't be fighting today," Bill says.

"I know, I just came to practice," I say.

"Good. Now go, then you can tell us about school," Bill says and I run off.

30 minutes later I was done practicing and I was sitting back at the bar.

"So, how's school kiddo?" Jack asks.

"Meh. Same old. I have a boyfriend though," I say with a smile.

"You do now. Who is he? What's his name? Is he a bad perosn? Does he do well in school?" Jack and Bill ask. I laugh and shake my head.

"Guys! Chill! It's Josh! No he's not a bad person and yes he's doing well in school!" I say. They relax.

"Good. Well we're happy for you," they say and pat my back. I thank them. I check the time and sure enough it was time for me to head back.

"Well I gotta go. If the guys catch me here they'll-" but I was cut off by a familiar voice.

"Kill you?" Mike says. I turn around and see all three boys smirking and have there arms crossed.

"Damn," I mutter and smile innocently.

"What are you doing here Princess?" Josh asks stepping closer to me.

"Uh uh...guys I didn't fight! Honest! I just practiced. I'm fine! Seriously! No need to be worried!" I exclaim.

"No need to be worried? Princess you almost died. Of course we're worried!" Josh exclaims but softens his voice once he see's I really was fine.

"He's right Lila. You should have waited a while. But since you're here, we can't stop you. But it's time to get back home so come on," Zack says. I sigh and look at Bill and Jack who were smirking and nodding their heads as if approving of the guys. I chuckle.

"See you later you two," I say and hug them. They hug me back and we depart. We walk to Mike's car and we drive off. Josh and I were in the back holding hands. Mike was dropping Zack off first.

"Bye guys. And Alisha, stay out of trouble okay? See you later!" He says and walks into his house. We pull out of the driveway and head back to our place. When we get out of the car, we saw 4 people sitting at our porch.

"Who are y-" Mike starts but I cut him off.

"RIPPERS?!" I screech.

Their heads instantly shot up and they ran towards me. Danger was the first one to hug me.

"God damn it Dy! I've missed you!" She says.

"I've missed you too D," I say.

"Little sis!" Chris exclaims and I run over to hug him. We embrace and he kisses my head.

"How have you been?" The twins ask at the same time. I hug then both and answer.

"You know same old. Other then the fact I just got out of the hospital, got an amazing boyfriend and made up with some friends, the same," I say with a shrug.

"HOSPITAL?" Chris exclaims.

"Friends?!" The twins yell.

"BOYFRIEND?!??!?!??!?" Danger shrieks.

I nod.

"Hospital? Why?" Chris asks sternly.

"Rebecca went over the limit. She's in jail chill," I say.

"Friends. Who?" The twins ask.

"Zack and Nina," I say.

"BOYFRIEND?!" Danger shrieks again.

"Oh yeah...Um...Josh," I say and as if on cue he wraps his hands around my waist and kisses my cheek.

"Oh....M....G!!!!!! You guys owe me 50 bucks each!" Danger yells in victory at Chris, Edward and Ray!

"What?" I ask.

"We made a bet that Josh would finally grow some balls and ask you out by the time we came to visit," Danger explains. I laugh. I guess Danger is getting 150$.

"Oh by the way, Josh," Danger says and the Rippers walk over to Josh pushing me aside.

"You hurt her," Chris starts.

"You die," the twins say.

"And that's a freaking promise," Danger concludes.

"Ok guys chill. He's a good guy, you've scared him enough," I say and walk over to Josh.

"Hey! Can we go inside now?" Mike asks. Wow, I completly forgot he was here.

"Yeah, come on," I say.

We go in and sit in the living room. Chris, Ray and Edward were sitting on the big couch and Danger was sitting in Chris's lap. Hmmm interesting. Mike sat on the small couch and me and Josh sat on the other small couch. Well he sat, I sat on his lap.

"So, why did you come back so early? It hasn't even been 6 months let alone 2 years!" I exclaim.

"Do you not want us here?" Danger asks with a smirk.

"D, you know that I want you here," I say.

"Yeah yeah I know. Anyways, we wanted to see how you were doing," Chris answers.

"Oh, well I'm fine. Obviously. How about you guys?" I ask.

"We're fine. Paris is great," Edward says.

"So...what's going on between you and D, Chris?" I ask with a smirk.

"Oh...you know," he stammers.

"Wait! I wanna guess! You guys went to the Eiffel Tower at night, you looked into each others eyes and kissed. Then you grew some balls and became girlfriend and boyfriend," I say.

"Wow, you're a good guesser," Chris says. I smile and shrug..

"I try," I say with a laugh.

We all laugh and continue to talk. The Rippers got to know Josh and Mike and Josh and Mike got to know the Rippers. I think my life has taken a twisted turn of events....for the better of course.

Epilogue

Alisha's P.O.V

Its been 7 years. Yes that's correct because I'm 23. 7 years and Josh and I are still together. Lets recap shall we?

After the whole me coming home from the hospital and Josh and Mike meeting the Rippers, they left 2 days after for Paris once again. I was sad but not was much as the first time.

A few weeks later, it was the end of the year and Mike graduated. After 4 days of convincing, he left for Washington DC for university. Josh ended up moving in with me permanently and let's just say the innocent good girl I was back then, wasn't so innocent in senior year. If you know what I'm saying. And if you don't, I didn't get pregnant at the age of sixteen, calm yourself.

Life carried on and Josh and I graduated together. Sure there were some ups and downs, and we did have a break up...that lasted a week, until he came into my room and we talked and kissed, and made out, and some other stuff which I'm not going to get into because I think you undertand. And if you still don't...starts with s ends with x. Get it?

Once we graduated I went to Harvard for medical, and thank heavens, Josh got in for Buisness. We got an apartment close to the University and you know, did bad things.

He proposed the day of graduation. I was so happy I ended up crying for days. Happy tears of course. We had our wedding at the age of 22 so it's been a year. I became a pediatrician and Josh runs his own company.

Lets move on to Mike shall we? Once he left for University, he met a girl named Lilly. She is so nice! Taned, tall, brown hair, hazel eyes. They went out for 4 years until my brother finally grew some balls and proposed. I was so happy for them! I ended up being her maid of honour and Josh was his best man. Mike became a lawyer and Lilly became a veterinarian because she loves animals.

As for Zack, well he found a girl. Her name is Becky. She has blonde hair and blue eyes and is so pretty. She is a little cocky, and stuck up, but I don't mind her. I mean, Zack can do so much better, but if he's happy I'm happy. They live in Hollywood togther because she's a model and has her fashion shows there. I meet up with him occasionally but he is always busy with work; he's a director. They aren't married, thank god, but I think they will be soon.

Now let's not forget about the Rippers. Chris and Delilah ended up getting married when Danger was 19 and Chris was 20. Young, I know. But they were happy and they loved each other. He proposed in front of the Eiffel Tower. Chris became a perfessional fighting teacher and Danger became a grade 4 teacher. They have a kid named Marcy and she's adorable! I mean, she is only 2!

The twins both got "hot chicks" as they put it. They are both Victoria Secret models and personally they aren't so bad. I've met up with them, Liv and Darcy. They are both my age and when they aren't on the runway, they eat like pigs. I swear to god, but the next day, they excersise for 5 hours straight to burn all those calories. Models I tell you! Both Ray and Edward decided to become models because they are "hot" and they decided they might as well "show off their bodies"...as they put it.

Oh we can't forget about Nina and Ally! Well, Ally had a secret boyfriend named Julien. He is a poet and an upcoming, famous writer! Ally decided to pursue her dreams of music and become a musican. She awesome!

Nina on the other hand, didn't have a happily ever after. She had a summer fling after graduation which ended up leaving her pregnant at 18. She told the guy, who's name is Mark, and he left her in an instant. He said he wanted no part in the baby's life and to never reach out to him. She was devasted but decided to keep the baby. She is now a single mother living in North Carolina as a waitress. She lives in a small apartment and I think she has a thing for a guy name Dan. Her baby, Margo, is 8 years old and is very happy. She may not be rich but she has an awesome mother and great friends.

And of course, the one and only, Rebecca. This is actually quite funny. When she went to jail she had high hopes her wealthy daddy would come and bail her out. That did not happen. Instead her parents left her there to "teach her a lesson". She was in jail for 5 years and ended up not graduating high school. So as a 21 year old, she went to high school to finish it off. She begged her parents to be home schooled or to do online classes but they refused. Something about humiliation and whatnot. Anyways, now she is working as a maid for a family far far away. We haven't heard from her since the 11th grade.

So that's how out lives turned out. We are all happy, except for Rebecca, and excited to see what our future hold next. All I know is that even with the pain and misery I went through in middle school and high school, I'm proud of my achievements. I had learned to accept the fact that Stacey was gone and it wasn't my fault, and I had learned that not everyone will leave you in life and that love does exist.

Oh! I almost forgot about some people! Mom and dad! I haven't really spoken to them. They've still been distant. They have never really understood and accepted the fact that their first daughter was gone, and because of that, they lost me and Mike. I'm pretty sure they are in Virginia right now. I don't talk to them much, but every now and then they send a postcard. The last time I saw them was at my wedding, a year ago.

As for the Underworld, well Bill and Jack say everything is running well, and I'm glad.

My life has been filled with many dverntures and I still can't believe I found the love of my life! Which reminds me...I have something to tell him.

"Hey! Babe!" I call though the apartment.

"Yes Princess!" He says and comes into the room. I sigh and sit down and he follows.

"What's up honey?" He asks. I look into his eyes and smile.

"I'm pregnant," I whisper.

His eyes bulge out of his sockets.

"You're-you're," he stammers, I nod happily.

"Oh my god! I'm gonna be a daddy!" He screams and picks me up and spins me around. I laugh and he sets me down on the bed. He lays down and I straddle him.

"I love you," he says. I smile and kiss him on the lips before whispering,

"I love you, too,"

The End

Milton Keynes UK
Ingram Content Group UK Ltd.
UKHW020317021124
450424UK00013B/1306